PRAISE FOR

JUST WRECK IT ALL

"Refreshing to see a story where there is no fat-shaming and no 'weight loss = salvation' message. . . . Moving."
—SCHOOL LIBRARY CONNECTION

"A much-needed story about a fat girl that does not equate weight loss with salvation."
—KIRKUS REVIEWS

"A heartfelt journey through the importance of self-love and forgiveness, perfect for fans of Sara Zarr and Gayle Forman."
—SCHOOL LIBRARY JOURNAL

"This refreshingly different plot manages to address current social concerns, such as body image, PTSD, domestic abuse, and small-town high school politics, with energy and unsentimental compassion."

Also by N. Griffin

The Whole Stupid Way We Are

JUST WRECK IT ALL

N. Griffin

A Caitlyn Dlouhy Book

atheneum   New York   London   Toronto   Sydney   New Delhi

atheneum

An imprint of Simon & Schuster Children's Publishing Division
1230 Avenue of the Americas, New York, New York 10020
For information about special discounts for bulk purchases, please contact Simon
& Schuster Special Sales at 1-866-506-1949 or business@simonandschuster.com.
The Simon & Schuster Speakers Bureau can bring authors to your live event. For
more information or to book an event, contact the Simon & Schuster Speakers
Bureau at 1-866-248-3049 or visit our website at www.simonspeakers.com.
Also available in an Atheneum hardcover edition
The text for this book was set in Scotch FB Text.
Manufactured in the United States of America
First Atheneum paperback edition October 2019
10 9 8 7 6 5 4 3 2 1
The Library of Congress has cataloged the hardcover edition as follows:
Names: Griffin, N., author.
Title: Just wreck it all / N. Griffin.
Description: First edition. * New York : A Caitlyn Dlouhy Book/
Atheneum, [2018] * Summary: "Crippled with guilt after causing a horrific
accident two years earlier, sixteen-year-old Bett's life is a series of pluses and
minuses. But when the pluses become too much to outweigh the minuses, Bett
is forced to confront her self-harming behavior"— Provided by publisher.
Identifiers: LCCN 2018008167 * ISBN 9781481465182 (hardback) *
ISBN 9781481465199 (paperback) * ISBN 9781481465205 (eBook)
Subjects: * CYAC: Guilt—Fiction. * Compulsive eating—Fiction. *
Eating disorders—Fiction. * Overweight persons—Fiction. *
Self-mutilation—Fiction. * High schools—Fiction. * Schools—Fiction.
Classification: LCC PZ7.G88135934 Jus 2018 * DDC [Fic]—dc23
LC record available at https://lccn.loc.gov/2018008167

For Kristin, because of the bus wish

JUST WRECK IT ALL

PROLOGUE

TWO YEARS AGO . . . More metal more dust more dirt, bursts of propane fire tongues leaping up and above Bett's head. So hot, so much *heat*. Hands underneath her rising Bett up then strapping her down and rising her up again until she was inside a cave no not a cave—a truck a van an ambulance?

Where was Stephanie? *Where was Stephanie?!*

Was that the school bus? How could Bett get on? Was she even alive?

How had she done it? How had she exploded and destroyed the world? The metal, the heat, oh God, Stephanie's blood—it was all Bett's fault and she would never get over it, never, if she even lived.

PART ONE

1

Autumn, Now, Thursday Morning, the First Day of Eleventh Grade

STANDING AT THE BOTTOM OF THE ROCKY PATH that led up to where Bett and her mother lived now, standing there at seven horrible thirty in the morning, Bett wasn't sure which kids would be on the bus heading her way, but that didn't matter. She knew she'd know them all. Salt River was large in land area but small in population, and Bett and her mother had stayed within the town boundaries when they moved this summer. And the truth was, any kid filled Bett with terror and anxiety, with their looking at her and their thinking their thoughts.

Bett's own thoughts raced. *Better if it's boys on the bus? Or girls? Boys. No, girls.*

Oh, neither. Why did I wear shorts?

Could she quick go back up the hill and change into jeans? But all Bett had time to do was stand there and worry, one hand clasping her opposite arm at the elbow, because the bus was heaving into view in front of her, diesel-stinking and loud. The folding door opened. Bett looked up. Driver's fist on the handle that opened the door. Bett stared at the driver. The driver stared at her.

She recognized him at once, thickset and sketch-looking with grayish hair and a stained baseball cap on his head. Eddie Pisca.

It was clear Eddie recognized her, too, and he must have read her thoughts. "Yeah. It's me. Two jobs. This and the vet center. Mind-blowing."

Then his face reddened. Bett knew why and the knowledge pulled all her own thoughts about being fat to the front of her mind again and brought with them the beginnings of tears.

Calm down, idiot! she told herself. *Stop it right now! Be reasonable.* Eddie hadn't seen her in years, couldn't know she was even fatter now than she had been when school ended last June. And that had already been super fat.

But there he was, staring at Bett with eyes that had some kind of film on them.

"So you're the girl who lives up there?" He nodded toward the slope. "The girl going to the school?"

Bett nodded back.

The red was fading from Eddie's face. "Then get the hell on my bus."

Bett got the hell on his bus.

The first person she saw was Dan, a skinny redhead with chin whiskers and an Adam's apple with a zit on it. He glanced up, then nodded hello at her.

But Bett couldn't nod back, even though Dan was an okay-enough kid. He was kind of techy and did a lot with the wood- and metal-shop crowd. The next person on the bus, also a boy, was staring out the window. Mutt. Ugh. Mutt was an ass, but at least she didn't see any of his friends on the bus. Mutt was always worse with a crowd, the kind of kid who threw Kool-Aid on you the day you wore white pants in the fifth grade. He was just the teen version of that now. He looked as if he were made of meat, like what people thought of when they thought of a movie high school boy.

The last kid on the bus was also a boy, smaller with tufty brown hair, bent over sideways with one arm stuck in his backpack, eyes on the ceiling as he rummaged around. He looked too young to be in high school, so he must be the lone junior high schooler on the bus, maybe seventh grade. Mutt and Dan were going into eleventh, like Bett.

No girls. Good. Right? Oh, I don't know!

Bett's face grew warm. She spent hours cutting up old men's jeans into shorts like these, shredding them just so and squeezing them over her thighs and butt. Her sweater was just as bad as the shorts. It had been the ugliest one in the thrift shop, which made her put it back on the rack at first because did its ugliness actually make it cool? But then she had seen it again for what it was, mannish and hideous, and had plunked down her three dollars and taken the sweater home with her. Wearing it today was a good proactive act against any positive thing she might do or imagine later—anything too Plus, as Bett thought of it. A Plus was any good feeling or action, and there was no Plus Bett would let herself countenance, not once she had recognized it as one.

"Sit somewhere in the first five rows," said the bus driver loudly. His face was reddening again, too. Why? Was it because he could see her rear in his mirror? "No one sits in the back of my bus. There've been incidents."

Incidents?

But Bett obeyed and passed Mutt where he sat behind Eddie and took a seat four rows back for herself. She sat down cautiously because what if something awful happened, like her sitting down made the seat rip? All these eyes on her were horrible enough.

"And buckle up." The bus driver shifted the bus into gear. It pulled away from the side of the road and heaved itself forth as the bus driver glanced at her in the mirror to make sure she did up the buckle. Despite the heavy sweater, Bett was freezing. Who'd have thought it would already be this cold in September?

"BETT!" shouted the bus driver.

Bett jumped. So did the boys.

"Jesus," said Mutt, sitting ahead of her with his gaze still fixed out the window.

"That's her *name*, guys," said the bus driver.

"We know," said Dan. "Bett's not, like, new-new."

"Are you going to scream at us all year again, Eddie?" asked the smaller boy. Now that he was out of his knapsack and she could see his whole face, Bett saw it was Dan's little brother, Ranger, with the same oval-shaped head and the same eyes as Dan, but brown-haired and smooth-skinned. He had found a plastic knife and fork in his bag and was using the knife to somewhat ineffectively peel an apple, eating the slices of skin as they fell into his lap.

"Yeah," said Eddie. "I am. Unless you clowns have gotten your acts together over the summer. Which you have not." He picked up speed and the bus lurched around the corner. Bett jostled unevenly in her seat.

"I'm pretty much the same," Ranger admitted, swallowing a piece of apple peel. "I tried out new ways to be interesting, but it hasn't really worked outcakes yet."

Outcakes? Bett cocked her head and looked at him. He looked back at her.

"Shut up with the 'cakes,' Ranger," said Dan, but Ranger did not shut up.

"Nocakes," said Ranger, eyeing Bett. "I'm testing it out. It's my new thing."

"Jesus!" said Mutt, louder this time.

"Why do you do this?" Dan asked Ranger. "Why do you find new ways to be an ass? Why don't you shave off the ass parts of you instead of, like, developing them?"

"I'm not an ass. Shut up," said Ranger, glancing sideways again at Bett. He blushed. "Cakes," he added defiantly and finished the last of his peel. "What do I do with the rest of this?" he asked the bus at large, holding his denuded apple between thumb and forefinger.

"Same thing you did last year with all them wasted apples. You wait until you get to school and drop it in a proper receptacle." Eddie shook his head.

"I think the flesh is grosscakes," Ranger said.

"Who raised you kids?" Eddie asked, tilting his head toward them but keeping his eyes on the road. "You got a new girl there, I tell you her name and not one of you introduces yourself."

"We have known her since *kindergarten*," said Mutt, voice strident now, though his eyes were still focused out the window. The bus route ran along the river, which was high today and rushing around the rocks studding its stream. The houses they passed were old, with cars out front with missing wheels, rusted swing sets on the side lawns. Bett rubbed her wrist.

Ranger furrowed his brow, considering. "Wait. You're kind of right, Eddie. I don't know her really much. Sorry."

"So tell that little girl your name right now!"

Ranger's brow furrowed further. "What little girl?"

Bett slid down in her seat.

Dan groaned.

It was the "little girl" that threw Ranger, Bett knew. Why couldn't she stop eating all the time? But she couldn't. Stopping was worse. No, not-stopping was. Oh, she couldn't think about that now.

Ranger finally turned to Bett. "I'm Ranger," he said. "Dan here is my brother. Cakes."

"It doesn't work if you don't make it a real suffix," said Dan. "It just sounds like a word you're saying, otherwise. Wait, why am I giving you *tips*?!"

"You're rightcakes!" said Ranger. "I have to wait until it's a habit. Thankscakes."

"Besides, I think everyone else got done with the 'cakes' thing about a hundred years ago, Ranger. You sound like Mom trying to be cool."

"I'm doing 'cakes' differently," said Ranger. "I mean like, real actual cake."

"What the hell are you even talking about," said Mutt. Although he was sitting, it was clear he'd grown even taller over the summer. He had wide-set eyes and a zit on his chin.

"NAMES!" screamed Eddie.

"She knows us!" yelled Mutt. He caught Bett's eye in Eddie's rearview mirror so she could see his mouth as he talked. "What the hell, Bett? In fourth grade you kicked my ass in hockey every time. You used to be an athlete."

Bett folded in her lips and blinked.

Her cheeks felt huge and her upper lip like there was a rim of grease on it, body nothing but a blob. *Don't you dare cry!* she told herself. *Don't you dare!* Sure, she had good hair, brown and thick and almost to her waist, but what was the point? She just jammed it into a fat messy bun on the top of her head every morning. She certainly knew how to do her makeup, but she never would, not since—no.

Ranger stared at Mutt. Then he stared at Bett. Then at Eddie.

"One more statement like that and you're off the bus, Mutt," said Eddie. "One more. I'm sorry some of these kids are buttwipes, Bett. I'm sorry they can't be trusted to open their damn mouths."

Bett swallowed and counted the scrapes on her legs from the sharp grasses that grew around the house she lived in now. If you could call it a house, given it was the size of a SIM card.

"I'll have you kids know that this is exactly why I'm thinking about having a silent bus this year," Eddie said.

"WHATCAKES?"

Mutt turned from the window again. "What the hell!"

"I mean it," said Eddie. "I'm not spending another year with bullshit."

"Silent, like, not even music?"

"Not even nothing."

"Mutt, say you're sorry!" Ranger urged.

"What do I care?" said Mutt. "I don't need to talk to you fools anyway."

"I don't care about talking," said Dan. "But I need music. Ban Mutt, Eddie, not music."

"The hell you don't care about talking," Eddie said. "You and your brother talk nonstop. Nonstop! All the time back there with your antics and semantics."

"No way," said Dan. "*Ranger* talks. I shut him up. I do, like, a service for you."

Eddie started drumming his thumbs on the wheel. "I'm trying to do this right," he said. "I'm trying to get your asses to that school in one piece and you behave like jerks."

"Hey!" said Ranger. "Not me! I was nice. Cakes," he added. "Nicecakes."

"Fine," said Eddie. "We'll do it this way. You can talk. Especially the girl. But not Mutt. Mutt, you're banned from talking. And no music for anyone. I never should've let you listen on here in the first place. Against school policy."

It was true. Salt River K–12 School had a ban on phones and music players during school hours on school property, but everybody brought them anyway—Bett's phone was in her backpack right now. People were pretty strategic about when they took them out, though, and usually buses were safe.

Bett took a deep breath in and exhaled as slowly as she could. Most boys in the high school were just longer, bigger-footed versions of the ones Bett had been on sports teams with for years when she was younger, right? All of them with bags of sweaty clothes and play-punching. She didn't do sports now, of course. No way. No—too *good*; too Plus. And physical action was the most Plus of all, so of course Bett would never let herself do anything like a sport.

Mutt, though. The pre-bus anxiety pit in her stomach grew until Bett couldn't bear it, couldn't wait for the end of the day and home.

She might be able to fix it if she were home.

"At least put on the radio," pleaded Dan.

"No," said Eddie. "I hate all that crap you kids listen to." His hand shot out and bashed the bus stereo's on button.

There was a two-part moan from Dan and Ranger, but it was too late.

The Eagles.

"Eddie," Dan said plaintively. "This is, like, *vintage*. It's a *cassette*."

"In the lah-ahng run . . . ," The Eagles sang, and Bett felt like she was trapped in the car with her own mother and Aunt Jeanette. Who could stand this eighties crap? The awful singing. The painful way the vocalists replaced every vowel sound with "ah."

". . . we'll fahnd out . . . in the lah-ahng run . . ."

Awful. More so because before she could cut off the thought, Bett was imagining herself taking a long run and getting away from these kids and the spectre of school,

14

jumping off this bus even as the sun hid behind a cloud and it began to rain on the windows, a sharp, bleak rain she imagined slicing into her face but she wouldn't care. Anything was better than this morning and that music and the smell of this bus, wet and moldered over in the new September raw. But that was the point. Bett knew she'd never do it. She hadn't let herself run in forever. And even just thinking about it was another Plus she would have to undo later.

Even though Eddie had just threatened them about their phones, Bett couldn't help it. She slipped her phone out of her bag and put one earbud discreetly in her right ear, the good ear, the one that didn't go out all the time like a bad stereo speaker.

Bus, First Day of Eleventh Grade, Bett with Her Phone

YOU HAVE TO LOOK, SHE TOLD HERSELF, THE WAY SHE told herself every time. *You have to.*

She brought YouTube up on the screen and typed in the familiar channel name, taking care to keep the phone well down below the bus seat in front of her so no one else could see. And there they were, the playlist of videos, each one a stab in Bett's wrist and the soles of her feet.

When she tapped play on a video, the shot panned around the room, the dolls everywhere. Creepy beautiful, enough to make a shiver run through her. There was a mermaid with wings. A goth girl with living flowers woven in her hair. A tiny one that looked as if she were made of stone. The camera moved to a table covered with fabrics and glue and strips of metal and foil.

Then the girl spoke. "This is what I do," she said. "I can't help it. It's, like, a compulsion. I'm going to show you how I do it."

RAYFENETTA, the screen said at the end. Rayfen was close by, just the next town over. Rayfenetta was just a play on its name.

3

Autumn, Thursday Morning,
First Day of Eleventh Grade,
Still on the Borderline Insane Bus

DAN CAUGHT BETT'S EYE AND RAISED A BROW AT HER.
She took the earbud out of her ear, slipped her phone back
into her knapsack, and looked down.

"Fine, Eddie," said Dan, turning back to the driver.
"What you've got playing here is great. I mean, I totally dig
it. A song with boredom's time signature, three chords, and
a beat like an old man's dying heart."

"Who asked you?" said Eddie, and turned up the sound.

"This sucks." Mutt shoved a huge hand into his pack
and, like Ranger before him, rummaged around, red-faced
and determined.

"Come on, Eddie!" cried Ranger, his red T-shirt hanging baggy over his skinny chest and stomach. Mutt's hand
reemerged from his backpack, triumphant, clutching

his own phone. "You're paid with our taxpayer dollars!" Ranger continued. "You have to let us have a say! Cakes!"

"Some people already eat more damn cake than they should," said Mutt, looking straight at Bett in the mirror again.

Second fat insult of the morning and she wasn't even at school yet. This time, tears did rise in Bett's eyes before she could stop them.

Eddie hit the brakes and the bus stopped short, right in the middle of the pothole-filled road. Bett's backpack fell on the floor, and all four kids flapped back and forth like licorice whips. Bett's lunchtime soda can shot down the aisle of the bus and smacked against the gearshift at Eddie's feet. Ranger's peeled, unwanted apple skidded to the front as well and lodged itself in the tangle of wires under the radio. The first aid kit trembled over the emergency fire hatchet in its glass case to the left of Eddie.

"Don't you talk to me like that," said Eddie to Ranger. "Your damn parents may pay money toward my services, but they do not pay for *me*. And *you* don't pay a penny for me to get you from your damn house to that damn school without killing you."

"I guess stopping short is your way of not killing us?" asked Dan, his voice compromised somewhat by the position of his head squashed against the seat in front of him. Bett rolled her head a little on her neck, testing. Should she go get her soda? No. Bett was not about to retrieve it right now, walking in front of Mutt, and open it only to have it explode all over.

"And you"—Eddie stabbed a finger at Mutt's reflection in the rearview mirror—"*you*, I have had it with, with your insubordination and insults. What kind of damn kid are you?" He opened his window, twisted in his seat, and, in one forceful arc, grabbed the phone from Mutt and flung it out the window. It landed in one of the dug-out basement holes that lined the side of the road across from the river. All this empty land used to be people's farms but had been sold off to become developments. COYOTE ACRES, the sign to this one said, but this development had stalled out at its beginning stages, leaving a long line of identical basement holes with stacks of planks piled in rows between them.

"HEY! That's my PHONE!" Mutt roared. "All my music is on that phone!"

Across the aisle, Dan opened and closed his mouth.

"Sue him!" yelled Ranger.

"The hell you will," said Eddie, and started up the bus again.

"That cost me a ton of money!" Mutt yelped.

"Then you should've kept it where it belonged," said Eddie, and the bus strained against its gears as it picked up speed. Bett couldn't help but be relieved that Eddie hadn't seen her with her phone just minutes before.

"You can't just do that!"

"No. YOU"—Eddie stabbed into the rearview mirror

again—"can't just be an ass to people and break the damn rules whenever you want. Learn that."

They drove on. Then the bus stopped short again.

"Jesus!" Dan shouted.

Ranger's head bobbled back and forth like a doll's.

"What now?" Mutt yelped.

Eddie eyed him in the mirror. "Go get your damn phone."

"It's way back there!" said Mutt.

"Run, then." Eddie turned off the bus.

The silence was sudden, and Mutt stood up. Eddie wrenched the door open and gestured. "Be my guest. Go."

"You can still sue him if it's busted up or wrecked from the rain," said Ranger eagerly. "Sue himcakes!"

"Shut up," Eddie, Mutt, and Dan said in unison.

Mutt swore and leaped out the door and pegged it down the road.

We'll be late, thought Bett, half fascinated, half scared.

"Hope he knows which pit," muttered Dan. But Bett's eyes were on Mutt. She couldn't believe how fast he'd gotten. Salt River was so small most teams were co-ed, and when they had been in elementary and junior high soccer and basketball, Mutt had been a very middling runner, definitely not your first choice to pass to. But now he'd already disappeared down the long dirt road. And just as quickly, he reared back into sight and onto the bus, damp with dirt all over and panting, but clutching his phone.

21

"Got it?" Eddie asked.

Mutt snorted.

"Good," said Eddie.

They waited. The bus was still.

"Are you going to take us to school?" asked Ranger. "Or are we, like, bus dwellers now?"

"Shut up, you," said Eddie. He crossed his arms over his steering wheel and his head dropped.

Why does every single person I know have to be completely weird? thought Bett. *Mom, Aunt Jeanette, now this bus driver.*

Eddie sat back up. "Okay," he said. Then, "Okay!" and he turned on the bus and threw it in gear.

"Never a dull moment in this vehicle," muttered Dan.

"Batshit," Mutt muttered as he dropped into the seat in front of Bett, still breathing hard. "What is wrong with him? Who does that?"

"Eddie," answered Ranger.

I want to go home, thought Bett, but that wasn't it. She wanted to go nowhere and noplace. All this time, taking so long, and she was tired of living through all its minutes.

TWO YEARS AGO . . . Up until the end of Bett's eighth-grade year, if you lived under some particular distance from the school, say like a mile, you had to walk to school instead of taking the bus. Bett didn't mind at all. In fact, she ran the whole way, her backpack full of a big night of eighth-grade homework making the run even better because it was harder, harder to take off, harder to fly down the dirt roads. Bett reveled in the difficulty of it, her muscles begging her to stop her flight, but . . .

You will not walk. You will run even faster.

And Bett did run even faster, loving the feeling of a too-hard run at the same time as hating the feeling of a too-hard run. The hate part of her run made the love part even better somehow. And the victory of having done that run before school even began, before other people were even up, or were just sitting voluntarily, doing nothing, made Bett feel completely badass, so badass she would have flown to that school with two backpacks on her back and one over each shoulder if she could have gotten away with it.

Speed, she wrote carefully on the bottom of her sneaker. Or Strong, or Light, or whatever quality she wanted in her running, so each step pounded the wishes into her body until the word was erased by the pebbles of the road shoulder and the idea was in Bett's feet forever. And there was no better feeling than after these runs. Which was good while it lasted because, she had found, expressions of pent-up body energy in school often made teachers, and, ultimately, principals, mad.

"You can't just run down these halls like they're your personal track, Bett," said the principal to her more than once.

"But they were empty," Bett pointed out.

"How do you know they would have stayed that way? How do you know that someone wouldn't have flung a classroom door open and smashed you in the face by mistake?"

That could happen if I were walking, too, head down like some stupid grackle eating pebbles. And I am not so dumb that I run along the walls where the doorways are. But she already had so many warning slips she knew she was just going to have to keep her mouth shut and eat this one, as she did the others.

But just as Bett was about to enter ninth grade, two things happened: 1) the school board read an article about how adolescents needed to sleep more, so they changed the time school started from seven thirty to eight for the junior high and high school kids, and 2) they lowered the distance that the bus would pick you up from one mile to a half mile. So now Bett was eligible to take the bus and her parents were making her take it.

"What? Why?!" cried Bett.

"You know why," said her mother, flipping the music from the seventies Simon and Garfunkel that Bett's dad had been playing to Led Zeppelin, her own favorite.

"We were home before, when you walked to school," said her father, watching her mother change the music as he leaned his skinny self against the sink to eat his cereal. "I was listening to that, Marianne."

"I can't stand that folksy shit," said Bett's mother. "And you used to love Zeppelin."

But Bett was too concerned with this bus thing to get involved in the music war. "I didn't *walk* to school," she said.

Her dad smiled at her. "When you *ran* to school. But with school starting later, we can't be home the whole time until you get there, and—"

"I'm not about to deal with a body-snatching," Bett's

mother, a policewoman, finished the sentence. "Especially of my own kid. Before, you could call me if any weirdass tried to get you, and I could be there in under a minute. But now I'll already be at the station house when you leave and so I'll be too far away to help. Forget it, honey. You're riding that bus."

"She could call either of us, Marianne," said her father, his spoon halfway to his mouth, his eyes still on Bett's mother.

Her mother snorted and rolled her eyes.

Bett broke the silence.

"I can outrun any weirdasses," she said.

"Don't you use language like that."

"It's what *you* just said!"

"*I* am an adult," said Bett's mother. "You can swear your face off when you hit eighteen, but not before."

This was so patently unreasonable that Bett said nothing.

In any case, this forced bus thing was no gift to Bett. Could she hold herself together until lunch break? In the eighth grade, in the junior high part of the school, she had been a force to be reckoned with in any of the softball or baseball or basketball games that sprang up at lunch or break time. And she needed that this year, too, she knew, but there was no way—ninth grade spelled the end of break time and lunch was just lunch, and you weren't allowed to go outside, not unless you were an upperclassman. And

Bett knew there was even more sitting once you got to the high school wing of the Salt River K–12 School. It was going to drive her nuts.

She'd have to use her old elementary school tricks. Ask to go to the bathroom, where she could swing on the door of the toilet stall, or jump and try to reach the rectangle of lights overhead, no fair starting the jump from the sink. Anything to get some of the pent-up feeling out before it built in her so much that if it burst, she'd shoot from the floor through the roof of the school like a ninth-grader-shaped rocket.

It was no wonder more of her friends had been boys than girls in elementary and junior high school since, face it, up to then there had been more boys than girls with her in those lunch-period games.

"Tell me about it," Bett's mother had said, more than once. "This is a man's, man's world." As a cop she knew what it was like to be one of the few female humans stuck in a confederacy of males.

But Bett didn't really care who she was playing with or against as long as she got to play, to run a puck down the ice with a hockey stick and whack it into a goal or to dribble dribble layup fly on the basketball court.

Bett was a beast.

Even for reasons not to do with being forced to sit instead of run to school, Bett wasn't crazy about buses. Field trips on a bus always smelled like a rubberized goods factory somehow and made her sick to her stomach.

I've got to distract myself from this, Bett thought on the bus the third day of ninth grade, holding her morning soda in her hand. *Okay. Divide this ride into three parts.* The first part of the ride to school was the way from Bett's driveway to a small horse farm. Not a farm for small horses—though how cute would that be?—but a farm that was small and had a few horses on it. Once the bus hit the end of that first stretch, Bett decided she was free to open the soda and slug a thirdsworth of the can down her throat. Then she'd wait until the second part of the ride, from that horse farm to a road crossing closer to the heart of town, to take her next thirdsworth of a swig. On one corner of that crossing there was a store sagging with flaky green paint where you could buy things like Cheetos and beef sticks and lottery tickets but also liquor in the back. The store was called Fancy Jim's. Bett had no idea why. She'd asked her dad ("Who knows?" he'd answered. "Maybe he named the store to reflect who he felt like he truly was."). Her father was always talking about things like reflecting who you felt like you truly were. *What else would you do?* thought Bett.

Opposite Fancy Jim's there was another farmhouse. That farmhouse was a mystery to Bett, and not only because she didn't know the people who lived in it— weird what with the town population being so small she could name practically everyone in it if you gave her five minutes—but because this farm was different:

a Christmas tree farm. And it did have adorable baby trees growing up in some of its fields, trees waiting to be old and tall enough to be in someone's house come some December. This house was also unusual in that it had three gas pumps in its front lawn, the middle one rusted and leaning to one side, and Bett had no idea why those pumps were there. The gas certainly didn't seem to be for sale—no high signs with prices per gallon, no car ever stopped in front of them that she had ever seen riding past to and from school. So she was free to make up her own explanations, which were:

> The house used to be a gas station, and the people who lived in the house now as a house couldn't be bothered to get rid of the pumps, or

> The house used to be a gas station, and the people who lived in the house didn't know *how* to get rid of the gas pumps, so the pumps just stood there in a row, like people waiting to be chosen for a softball team, or

> The people who lived in the house had put them there themselves as some kind of art project.

The last one occurred to her because more and more people from the city were moving up here and buying houses and coming on weekends. Bett and her mom saw them when they went into town. You could pick out the city people a mile away, with their carefully chosen country clothes and boots that had never seen mud. Or they were in athletic wear made out of complex fabrics, racing through the town in expensive sneakers. The city people walking on Main Street all beamed at the Salt River people as they passed and Bett knew this was because people like Bett and her mom and the actual citizens of the town were only background characters in the city people's life movie, this section of which was probably called something like *Country Livin'*. They would leave off the *g* in "living" because they would think that mimicked the rural accent of Salt River when they finally drove their huge, unneeded SUVs back into the city, where they'd come from, and Bett and the rest of the town relaxed, knowing they were no longer characters but belonged to themselves again, for better or worse, at last.

Anyway, the city people were also forever putting sculptures in their yards and trying to start events with names like ArtBeat! ("We want to bring culture to this town!" they cried on Town Meeting day, without caring that Salt River already had a lot of great stuff going on all year. Like the Agricultural Fair up at the school, so much fun in the fall with games and animals and treats in booths run by each class grade six and up, as well as the Winter Festival in December and then all the maple sugaring parties in the spring, with cider doughnuts and pickles to cut the sweet. Bett loved it all.) And you couldn't last through the long winter up here with no hobby to do in the dark hours in a snowbound house, so people who painted often had their pictures up in the coffee shop in town, which doubled as a deli, and in the insurance office and in the banks and even in the Veteran Services Center building, where Eddie and Bett's dad worked.

And when Salt River people wanted to have friends over, they just did, with minimal fuss and no discussion about the food beyond the organizational. Bett and her friends always left the adults immediately and went off and played Xbox until it got boring and then they went outside to talk down by the river, where they made piles of stones, sometimes, largest to smallest, or went toe-dipping into the freezing waters. Once they built a lean-to over one of the cairns but it didn't stay up. Not enough twine to tie it together. But that didn't matter. It was the making of it that was fun.

Sometimes they just sat by the shore, toying with Kelley's dad's cigarette lighter to see who was brave enough to palm the flame. Or they took turns sweeping a finger through the flame to see who came out unharmed. (Everybody. No one was stupid enough to let a finger rest in the path of the flame, except Mutt that one time, but that was only to show off in front of one of the girls, Hester or somebody, who he had a crush on.)

But Bett and her mother and her mother's friends didn't really care about the city people. This year was different at school, though, at least among the girls. Now, in ninth grade, some girls were considered to be the ones you were supposed to want to be like, and then there were the rest of them, like Bett, who were supposed to be ashamed of being the way they were. The first group leaned toward being more like the city people, while Bett and her friends were mostly in the Stay group.

Bett didn't know why "Stay" fit the feel of the group so exactly, only that it was mostly made up of people who somehow lived all the way in Salt River, in the farms and stores and the cop house, like her mother. Stay was brown and gray and green like tree bark and dirt roots and cow poo, and Salt River was all those things. But the other girls were making a new group that, like the city people, felt like it visited Salt River on feet that twinkled like stars, moving toward some life that Bett didn't get wanting. The Twinkler girls all seemed so confident. They wore makeup and the kind of clothes you were meant to wear like movie people and had hair that was done in A Way. And now some of the Stay group girls were baldly turning their backs on the other Stays, and the mud and dirt and animals of Salt River, and were forcing their way into the group of Twinkler girls, first by hanging out at the periphery of that group at their lockers and then by doing their own hair in The Way and using their babysitting money to

buy Twinkler kind of clothes and then, finally, boldly, set-
ting their lunches down at the Twinklers' table, where they
would sip one juice and eat just one item on their lunch
tray and throw away the rest. All the while they talked
like the Twinklers, as if they were trying to speak French
or something. From her own lunch table, Bett wondered if
the new, previously Stay Twinklers were as valued as the
Twinklers-from-the-start, and thought it unlikely. Because
if she was honest, even the Stay people had a weird hier-
archy to them.

Like we never talk to that girl with the dippy bangs cut
way back past her ears, and we don't talk to that boy who
reeks like his pig farm and doesn't notice he has so much
dirt under his fingernails it looks like he has some kind of
permanent reverse French manicure.

So, if you thought about it, Bett and the Stays, many
of whom also took care of pigs and cows, were no better
than the Twinkler group, whose always-Twinkler group
believed they were better than the previous-Stays. But
even if there were subgroups in both the Stays and the
Twinklers, it mattered less than the separation between
the two.

Wait, why was she thinking about the Stays and
Twinklers now, on this bus ride? Oh, right. Bett was waiting to take her second thirdsworth of a swig of her soda,
which she'd do when the bus turned right at Fancy Jim's
and the gas tank Christmas tree farm toward the center of

town and Salt River K–12, completing the semicircle that described Bett's ride to school. But they had been stopped at the road crossing forever. The third and last part of the ride was the longest and dullest one, but even so, if school was inevitable, why was Pat, the bus driver, stopping here? And delaying Bett's soda?

"Do you know why we're stopped?" Bett asked Paul, who was in her class and also a basketball beast.

"The Catholics?" he guessed.

"Oh, right." Bett remembered. There were so few kids in the Catholic school now that they couldn't afford their own buses, so the public school buses were taking the kids who needed to go to the Catholic school there, too. They started the year later than the public school kids, so today was their first day.

Bett held her soda gingerly, because, even though she had already taken her first swig, the soda was all stirred up from the bumping bus ride and she could feel it bubbling against the two fingers she held over the opening of the can. She released them the barest bit and fizz spilled over the lid, but not horribly, not to the point of mess-making. Bett licked it and took her second-third swig as a girl with a headful of long straight dark brown hair that could be considered done in The Way came down the aisle in a plaid skirt and blue sweater.

"Can I sit here?" asked the girl as she got to Bett's row. Bett shrugged and moved over, one hand holding her soda and the other hoisting her backpack on her lap to give this girl enough room.

"I'm just Catholic," said the girl beside her. "I'm not new or anything. So you don't have to worry about being stuck introducing me to your school."

"I kind of guessed that," said Bett. She glanced at the girl's sweater and skirt.

The girl caught the glance. "This foxy look is a dead Catholic giveaway, right?"

Bett snorted with surprise. The girl laughed, and then they caught sight of the contents of Bett's snort on the back of the seat ahead of them, and both of them laughed so hard and so long that no sound came out and the last part of the bus ride was over before they knew it because the laugh was as wide as a week.

The bus pulled up at the Catholic school and the two of them were still laughing.

The girl wiped tears from her eyes. "Save me a seat this afternoon," she said to Bett.

"You have to save one for me," said Bett. "With your weird Catholic shorter day."

"Fine," said the girl. "You just sit there wearing human clothes and be mad about the one good thing about going to my school."

They laughed again, but they were already weak from the last laugh, and the girl had to get off the bus with all her stuff, but it didn't matter because they were already friends. Bett didn't know a word for this instant familiarity you felt when you met someone who got it, whatever "it" was. But that's what happened between her and this girl.

Bett wondered what the girl's name was. *Whoops.*

5

Thursday Morning,
the Start of Eleventh Grade at Last
After That Wack Bus Ride

EDDIE PULLED THE BUS UP IN FRONT OF SALT RIVER K–12, and Ranger piled out, followed by Mutt and Dan and then Bett, who was full of anxiety again at the thought of seeing and being seen by everyone else out there. She was ready as could be expected for the rigors of eleventh grade, but the schoolful of kids boiling up the lawn was already too much. Especially after that crazy bus ride.

The school itself was old stone walls with large rectangular windows staring out at the lawn and stairs in the center leading to its main doors. Ahead of her, Ranger walked toward the entrance, tossing his head back every once in a while to keep his baseball cap out of his eyes, even as he kept hoisting his backpack over his shoulders. The double movement made him stagger sideways like a drunkard.

"You know where our homeroom is?" Dan asked Bett.

Bett opened her mouth wordlessly. *Speak.* "I can find it," she managed at last. She tugged her sweater down and briefly wished she could tug her shorts legs down as well, long enough to cover her whole bottom half. But no. This was the whole point of wearing them. Mortification was everything, everything Plus- and positive-preemptive.

Dan shrugged and let his steps take him a little ahead of her, behind his head-tossing little brother.

Oh. It was a question, not an offer. Bett was such an ass. Dan's own backpack was slung over one shoulder as he walked, hands in the pockets of his hoodie, head down and kind of bobbing as he headed into the school.

Mutt was ahead of her, too, already surrounded by his minions. "My dad's name is on that," he bragged to them now, nodding at the statue at the base of the school's stone steps. "IED in Iraq. Shrapnel still in the old man's skull. Too small to get out. And still he walks."

Bett glanced at the statue now, one that honored every-body in Salt River who had served in a war. It was a man holding two other men in his arms, the arms of those men dangling, their faces slack. It was beautiful, in a sad kind of way. Bett had grown so used to it, though, that the man supporting the other two seemed to her to be more a resting place for the crows that bobbed around the school entrance than a man. Bett stayed her course up into the entrance of the school, but she knew if she turned around that the back of the statue man's jacket was bulky, as if he had something under there. Supplies, maybe. He was a soldier, though, so more likely some kind of weapon.

Kids from all the buses piled into the school and swarmed forth to find their homerooms. Bett let them bump her and pass her on the way into the main foyer. The foyer itself was lined with charcoal drawings from the school's free summer art classes, portraits of people's grandparents, mostly, or other old people. They were surprisingly lovely. Who knew the proportion of kids who could draw was so high in Salt River? All Bett knew was that she certainly wasn't one of them. There had been the tree incident in grade four, when her homeroom teacher suggested she be the cleanup monitor of the class if she didn't feel successful as an artist. Fine by Bett. Why draw a thing when you could just be outside and look at it?

"You have the first lunch," Mrs. Schlovsky, the apricot-haired woman who ran the main office, told Bett as she handed her her schedule for the year.

"First lunch?" Bett groaned inwardly. First lunch was at the inhumane hour of 10:48 and full of kids from the junior high part of the school. Bett would stand out like a camp counselor surrounded by tens of Rangers. "Can I switch out?"

"Don't give me any grief," said Mrs. Schlovsky. "You kids have no idea how hard it is to put together these schedules. Besides, there are other juniors in that lunch, don't worry."

Ugh.

Bett exhaled. There was no more putting it off. She had to make her way up to the third floor and her own homeroom. She climbed the stairs and stood at the door, steeling herself to go in, glancing into the classroom to see who was already there. There was Dan, talking to Hester, one of the few brown girls in the school and the only one in the high school. Hester had been adopted by a white family when she was born, and she hated it when someone, usually a clumsy teacher, brought up race.

"Shut *up*," she would say to the class. "You people know nothing." And she was kind of right. Salt River was almost entirely, rurally, Northeastily white, and race was not exactly a common topic of conversation amongst the white people.

Anna was with Hester and Dan as well, she and Hester slim as those little stone tube houses the caddisflies built—you could find them in the river if you knew where to look. The girls' elbows were so thin they made points. A bunch of guys were tossing a Superball back and forth on the other side of the room, bouncing it against the ceiling and walls, getting it all in before the homeroom teacher showed up.

Bett slipped into the room and took a seat in the back as quietly as she could.

Crash!

Bett jerked. The Superball had slammed into the can of pens on the teacher's desk and tipped them to the ground. The noise was enough to make Bett's bad ear, the left one, fill with fluid and go out momentarily so the room quieted immediately by half. Anna leaped over to pick the pens up while the guys laughed like hyenas and high-fived each other and started up with the ball again, whipping it at one another with an aim to harm.

Slowly, Bett's ear settled and she took a pen out of her backpack and parked an ankle on her opposite knee. STOP, she wrote on the bottom of her sneaker. She traced the word until it was thick and black and depressed into the sole.

6

At Bett's Locker After Homeroom, First Day of School, About to Do an Illegal-on-School-Premises Thing

OKAY, BETT TOLD HERSELF, HIDING HER PHONE WITH her hand in her locker while she put in her one earbud with the other. *Now. You have to.*

And she pushed play on the Rayfenetta channel again.

"Blythe dolls are special," Rayfenetta was saying. "You can change out their hair and clothes and even their eye color."

Bett flinched.

But Rayfenetta was something else. You wouldn't believe what she could make out of those dolls, and not just by switching out their eyes.

What did Rayfennetta's *eyes look like?*

No. Don't think about that.

Yes. You have to.

Bett watched as hands in the video cut out tiny pieces of foil and made them into a flower. Then the hands set the flower to one side and started cutting out more pieces of something like the foil, only heavier and even more metallic; she was using some kind of clippers rather than just regular scissors. What was Rayfenetta going for? Whatever it was, the doll was already gorgeous, partially dressed in a bodice made of the metallic stuff, braided and cross-woven in a complex pattern of three interlocking triangles.

Rayfenetta put the clippers down and took up the scissors again, but what was she cutting? Bett leaned in close. There was the barest hint at the edge of the frame. It was hair. Rayfenetta's actual hair. There was a snip, and then a thin, five-inch hank of hair was in Rayfenetta's hands and she took up the doll and started braiding her hair into its.

Autumn, Thursday,
First Day of Eleventh Grade, Lunchtime

"HI, BETT!" IT WAS RANGER, STANDING IN FRONT OF her in the barbarically houred lunch line. "They got tater tots!"

How was this kid so cute? Seventh graders were generally not adorable. Though Bett imagined Ranger had it tough in his own way, in a class full of well-developed girls and boys who were taller than he was.

"Hi, Ranger," she managed to say back. At least she could talk to a seventh grader. "Congrats on the tots."

He beamed at her. "Totscakes," he said. "Want to cut me?"

Bett looked at him, startled, and then realized he meant in the lunch line. "Sure," she said. *Why not?*

It was as bizarre as she had imagined to sit with a

seventh grader at lunch. But Ranger seemed cheerful enough about it, even as the lunchroom filled.

"Bett. Dumbass." It was Dan, passing them with a loaded tray on his way with a couple of senior guys to another table. Neither of the other guys said a word to her as they passed, but that was fine with Bett as she remembered her weird sweater and shorts. The inner thighs of the shorts were already fraying from her legs rubbing together, so she was almost afraid of standing up to empty her tray when the time came. Maybe she could wait everyone out and be last to leave. Ranger, though. That kid was parked with her for the long haul.

Across the lunchroom, Anna, a born Twinkler if there ever was one, was tearing off tiny pieces of a roll with bony, slim fingers and slowly putting them in her mouth. She wore drapey, artily torn clothes over her stick arms and leggings on her stick legs. The group of girls she was with laughed continuously, one after the other, sometimes two, the sound trickling like water in a stream.

Behind Bett, a bunch of Mutt's minions were already seated. "He's so proud of his dad on that statue," said one now.

"So what?" said another. "My grandfather's on it and I'm proud of that."

"Yeah, but your grandfather isn't a dick. Mutt's dad is."

"What else is new?"

"He called Mutt a fag last night."

N. GRIFFIN

"So he's a homophobic dick. We knew that. Gimme your tater tots."

"And shut up. Here comes Mutt."

"It was in one of those goddamn *basement holes.*" Mutt was plonking down his own tray and clearly continuing a conversation he had started with them earlier, pissed off still and reliving the events of the morning bus ride. "You know what? I am so sick of people coming up here and wrecking the place with these new houses. They cut down all the trees so snowmobiling is no fun over there anymore. 'Coyote Acres.'" Mutt snorted. "There aren't even any coyotes left in those woods, anyway."

Bett's head came up, surprised. She had thought that kind of thing was her own personal Stay sort of observation. But she would never turn around and say so, not after Mutt's morning assholery.

She looked back down at her lunch tray, but on the way she caught Dan's glance. There was agreement in his brown eyes, agreement about Mutt's assholiness and the development both. Bett's face grew hot. She did not have moments with people at school.

"And then that anus of a bus driver—"

But Ranger was calling to his brother's table, a beat too late, really, to pick up on Dan's earlier insult: "I'm not a dumbasscakes!" and the moment ended, thank God, because Dan was calling back over to Ranger:

"DUMBASS. YOU ARE A DUMBASS. THAT'S

WHAT I CALLED YOU BECAUSE THAT'S WHAT YOU ARE," and all the noise of the caf blended with their argument, Ranger cakesing along and holding his own against the stream of Dan's disdain. Bett couldn't help but admire the kid's persistence.

Then: "I got to go to the bathroom," Ranger announced abruptly. God, he was young.

"Go, then," said Bett. "I'll let them know where you are if anyone asks." Now was the time for her soda, warmish and dented but still sweet. It was going to be an adventure, opening this can, given how it had been knocked around the bus this morning. Still, she was glad she'd picked it up off the floor on her way off her bus. Soda was her life's blood.

Through the windows, a group of seniors were kicking a soccer ball around, but gently, talking at the same time, none of the whip energy of the junior homeroom Superball pegging tournament. More like the ripple of a warm-up dribble with a field hockey ball or the bumping of a nineties-feeling hacky sack, which her father had been into but Bett had been spared from for the last two years.

But at least those kids were outside. At least they let themselves move.

Bett sniffed the air. Was that a whiff of smoke? There was a line of kids who sat with their backs to the school outside every lunch period, smoking cigarettes. Maybe the smell was drifting in from the open window of the caf. Or no, more likely the smoke was coming from the bathroom outside of the caf, where people also gathered to do their smoky thing. The stink was gross.

But before she could think about it more, Ranger was tearing back into the room, still doing up his belt buckle, the metal parts of it clinking together like a pair of stones.

Dan slapped his forehead with his palm.

"It's like the kid goes out of his way to be an idiot," he said to his friends.

But Ranger was clearly too worked up to care about his undone-up pants. "Come see!" he cried, and it wasn't just Bett who looked up. There was genuine alarm in his voice. "Come see!"

Bett left her lunch at her table and hurried behind a smallish crowd out into the main hallway behind Ranger. Once out in the hallway, she gasped along with the other kids who had followed Ranger out, too. Every drawing in the long front hallway had been slashed from top to bottom, the remains of the drawings swaying and swinging against the wall, pieces of faces dragging against the tiles, and those pieces were smoking, burning, fire licking and curling at the paper edges as if someone had walked by with a knife and a fingertip of flame.

"What the hell?" yelped Dan.

"Get out!" screamed a teacher. "Now!"

But kids weren't listening, instead shooting their water bottles at the flaming, smoking paper even as other teachers were now yelling at them. There was Mutt coming out of the caf, too, with his loud, meaty friends, stopping short in the cloud of smoke.

Mutt swallowed hard, staring at his own name on one of the drawings from the summer, hanging now in smoking shreds.

If the hallway hadn't been on fire and Mutt hadn't been such a douche this morning, Bett might have had brain space to feel bad for him. But she was too shocked at the weird rage of the fiery destruction going on here to think about anything else at all.

Then one of the pictures flared up in flames and the rest went up, too, in a roar, and the school fire alarm finally went off, sudden and loud. Bett ran outside the building with everybody else, past the statue of the man holding the other two, heart pounding, near to throwing up and her left ear completely out again and numb.

8

Thursday, End of the First Unexpectedly Flamey, Loud, and Unsettling Day of Eleventh Grade

"DO WE HAVE, LIKE, A PSYCHO IN OUR MIDST?" SAID Dan in p.m. homeroom. He was only saying what other people, Bett included, were clearly feeling. Wasn't the slashing and burning one of those signs they were always being warned about of someone who was about to go off on the whole school? Who even was it? A student who hated Salt River as much as Bett had grown to? An ex-student or a random nut who had not signed in with the apricot-haired office lady, as per procedure? Bett hoped it would be figured out quickly, today, because the last thing she needed was her own mother the cop up here investigating, for God's sake. But she knew that was probably inevitable.

And sure enough, just before the final bell, the principal

had to get on the loudspeaker to address all the nerved-up chatter about the sliced, burned drawings. "The police have been called and an investigation has been launched," he said sternly.

Oh, God, help me.

Bett's mother's uniform alone was enough to make Bett need to go lie down, never mind watching it walk around her own school with her mother inside it.

"We'll be questioning students in my office throughout the week," Mr. McLean, the principal, continued. "The person responsible will be caught."

But that didn't stop the murmur of fear and worry from the kids in the homeroom, or quiet the scared pit in Bett's own stomach. *What kind of whackjob does something like that? And boldly, right in the middle of the school day?* Bett's heart beat faster, and she tried to force herself to take deep breaths to slow it.

But the panic grew anyway, even though the fluid in Bett's left ear had settled a bit and she could hear pretty okay again.

Oh, why couldn't today have been like the first day of second grade, she thought, when you couldn't wait to use the unopened crayons, and everything had an added polish of newness? Eleventh grade, everybody knew, was the hard grade, the one that mattered most if you were going to go to college. All the Twinklers would go, and a handful of Stays, with some of the Stays going to the ag college in

Rayfen for the two-year farming program. But, instead of plans and academic stress, here was the year starting off with fear and flames.

The bell rang. Bett jumped a mile.

When she got on the bus after school, Mutt and Dan were already on.

"That Mutt is a good-looking kid," Bett's mother had said to her more than once. "That whole family is, cousins and uncles, with those wide-set eyes. Too bad so many of them are messes."

"Ugh," Bett had responded. "You always talk about their wide-set eyes. You make them sound like a family of haddocks."

"Well, they're sexy haddocks, then," Bett's mom had said.

"Mom! Gross! Mutt is sixteen! And an ass!"

"Jesus, Bett calm down. I didn't mean him." There was a pause. "I didn't know he was an ass. But he is a good-looking haddock. You have to admit."

"I do not," Bett had said, and she still agreed with herself now that she was on the bus.

"Hi, Bett, I'm Dan," said Dan loudly now, in his seat across the aisle from Bett on the bus. It was clearly for Eddie's benefit.

"You shut up," said Eddie. "I was just trying to see that you got manners. Jesus Christ."

Dan rolled his eyes.

Ranger clattered onto the bus now, his backpack unzipping itself, papers and new books coming out in terrible hanks.

"Ranger, you can't see with that hat," said Dan.

"Yes, I can," said Ranger. "I got, like, a slit of space underneathcakes."

"Ugh!" Dan shrank down in his seat.

But Ranger was already babbling on. "What do you guys think of the fire-slashing psycho?"

"Don't worry about the psycho," said Bett, startling herself by talking. But she didn't want a little kid like that to be scared, did she? "Here, let me help you."

She got up and stuffed papers back into Ranger's backpack, tipped his hat back on his head, and squared him away in the row in front of his brother, even though it left her rear end exposed to Mutt. But Mutt was so self-absorbed he was just looking at his own reflection in the window anyway.

"But for realcakes, what do you guys think about those ruined pictures?" asked Ranger to the bus at large.

"Totally sucks," said Dan. "And what the hell?" Or at least Bett thought that's what he'd said. Her left ear was going out again from all the din of the day, and that always meant she misheard things. Like once she was convinced the security guy in the airport was asking everybody to put their poetry in the bins. "I don't have any poetry," she had said to him, bewildered. "Toi-let-tries," the man sighed at her. But that mishearing had scarcely mattered. It sucked more in moments like now, when she couldn't follow the conversation around her and had to just wait and wait for her ear to settle down.

"Pointless," said Mutt, or so she guessed. He wasn't facing her, so she couldn't be sure. He surprised her, though, by joining the talk.

"Plus, who would, like, take the time to do that?" Dan asked.

"You kids don't know from psycho," Eddie said loudly enough for even Bett to be sure of what he was saying. "Go to Nam back in the day and I'll show you some psychos."

Bett didn't know what to think about that. She thought of the morning, and she remembered Eddie's strange volatility from when she was small as well and still bothered to visit her dad at the vet center. One time, for example, Eddie had hung up the phone after a difficult call at the desk and cleared the entire wall of pamphlets in two great bear-paw swoops, shouting all the while.

Salt River's Veteran Services Center was depressing as hell. Bett remembered that, too. Fake-wood-paneled walls lined with peeling posters hung too high and all those pamphlets, faded and curling at the corners. Still, Bett assumed Eddie liked the center and the people there, even if her father was a twiddly little shit. There were other people who worked at the Veteran Services Center who were not asses. But some of the old, little-kid fear from that pamphlet-flinging day licked at Bett's mind now, and her nervousness about Eddie mixed with the day's fears about the fire and knifing.

Eddie threw the bus into gear now and they were off, the bus tracing the other semicircle of its route toward Bett's house. That was the deal in Salt River. You might get to sleep later and be one of the last ones on the bus, but that meant you were also one of the last ones off the long, long route in the afternoon, which was a drag. Still, Bett would rather sleep later than get home early, especially to her weird, teeny house, where her mother was everywhere. At least there were no Catholic kids on this bus to make the route longer—

No. Bett cut herself off. *Don't think about that.*

At last, Mutt dropped off on Field Road and Dan and Ranger at the corner of Kunst Street and Bett the last one on the bus, Eddie pulled up to the slope leading to her house and she gathered up her own things and climbed down the three steps to the ground.

"How'd it go?" Eddie looked down at her, his fist on the bus door lever. "You worried about this stupid nut with the fire, too? Don't be. You twerps will be fine."

Eddie paused, waiting for her to respond. But Bett could not. Eddie stared at her.

Then, Plus or not, Bett couldn't take it and she had to turn and run up the slope, away from Eddie's gaze, the backpack on her back making the weight on each foot about a trillion too-Plus pounds.

Behind her, Eddie finally pulled away.

TWO YEARS AGO . . . Stephanie Roan, which turned out to be the name of that ninth-grader girl from the Catholic school on the bus with Bett, was something else. She was good at art and wild in her hopes and ways of talking. "I want to do makeup for the movies," she told Bett as they careened toward their separate schools on the bus in the morning. "I have a ton of it. And I am going to practice on you."

"I think you could do better," said Bett, taking her second soda swig as the bus started to jounce its way along that last part of the ride that particular January day. The town was full of snow now, which was glorious because it meant flying across that snow and ice, sheening or playing ice hockey or cross-country skiing.

"Snobface," said Stephanie, and she really looked hurt.

"No!" said Bett. "I meant you could pick a better face to practice on."

"No way," said Stephanie, and stuck one arm deep in her knapsack. "You have this thing where you're pretty and you don't know it. I'm getting out my makeup bag."

But in the end it didn't matter because the bus bounced and the eyeliner Stephanie was using on Bett's eye slid down Bett's cheek like an ancient Egyptian tear, and once again she and Stephanie were laughing so hard they banged back and forth in their seats until the laughing was too much for sound and went quiet.

Every other Wednesday was a half day at both schools for teacher meetings, and one Wednesday, one of the few when Bett didn't have to stay after for some kind of sports practice, Stephanie grabbed Bett's arm when she sat down on the bus and said, "Get off with me at my house. We can hang out and then your mom or dad can pick you up on their way home from work."

Bett hesitated. She knew she should call her mom for permission, but somehow she didn't want to do that in front of Stephanie. Wasn't she fourteen and old enough to live her own life?

"Okay," she said. "Fine." And when the bus stopped at Stephanie's house, Bett flew off with her, Pat the bus driver not even demanding a note.

*　*　*

"I have to ask you something, Steph," said Bett. She was hesitant, because although Stephanie lived on a farm, if Bett was honest, the private school and the movie makeup thing made Stephanie a potential Twinkler, and Bett didn't want to make a Stay–Twinkler divide between them when they were such good friends, even if only on the bus. Which was a little weird, when you thought of it. Bett and Stephanie had so much fun together on those rides, but neither had been to the other's house or invited the other to any parties or hangouts with friends from their respective schools. It just hadn't seemed right. Or maybe Bett and Stephanie both liked that it was just the two of them with nothing outside to mess anything up. They were uncomplicated bus friends, and here was Bett, about to fly through that Venn diagram of their bus and non-bus lives and maybe land in Stephanie's yard and sort of wreck it all, and this question was going to be the first step toward that destruction.

"Okay," said Stephanie. Bett saw she was clearly braced for something awful, like did Stephanie know she had a zit on her nose or what was up with all her freckles.

"It's nothing big," Bett hastened to say. "I just want to know about the gas pumps."

Stephanie looked puzzled. "What about them?" she asked.

"Well, like, why do you have them?"

Stephanie looked at Bett like Bett was daft. "We have a lot of tractors and backhoes and stuff on this farm," she said. "Easier to have the gas here than to have to drive into town all the time."

Bett was so happy that the pumps weren't a sculpture that she laughed. She laughed until Stephanie kicked her in the foot.

"Are you laughing because I live on a Christmas tree farm?" Stephanie was ready to be pissed.

"*No*," said Bett, laughing again. "I just thought they were . . . I thought they were an—" She laughed until Stephanie kicked her on the shoe again.

"What?" Stephanie asked. "Tell me, moron."

"An art project," Bett said at last, wiping tears from her eyes.

Stephanie stared at her. "You mean like that naked woman made out of metal in that pervy guy's front lawn down by the hair place? Or all those green shapes that lady welded together in front of the library and named *Love's Mercy*?"

Now Bett was laughing so hard she couldn't talk, but Stephanie kept on, her voice threaded through the laugh that was about to come. "You thought maybe my family got together over *lattes* and decided that we'd do our own sculpture and it would be three ancient gas pumps? Do you not get us at all, Bett?" But by the time she got to "get," Bett couldn't even understand the rest of the sentence because they were both laughing so hard, real laughing, like on the bus, only they weren't on the bus and that was wonderful because the burst Venn diagram hadn't wrecked their world after all.

Their laughing hadn't fully calmed down until they had dumped their backpacks in Stephanie's kitchen and come back outside into the cold January air.

"Let's go into Fancy Jim's for a soda," said Stephanie. "You had one on the bus, but I'm thirsty."

"I offered to share," Bett protested. It was true. The ride home described the same half circle made by the morning route and Bett had a soda for that one, too, every day, and always offered some to Stephanie.

"Well, you drank it all, and now I want one. From Fancy Jim's."

"Stephanie, we cannot go into Fancy Jim's."

"Why not?"

"Because it's FANCY JIM'S!" Bett's mother the cop had warned her more times than she could count to stay away from that place.

"Full of troubled people," her mom had told her.

"I thought you said most troubled people were more sad than scary," Bett had pointed out.

"That's right. Most. But not all. And God knows what else happens in that store."

It was easy enough to avoid Fancy Jim's because, although she passed the place every day on the bus, Bett had rarely been directly outside of it in person, with its flaking paint and slanted door.

But here she was now, in the Fancy Jim's parking lot that had just one blue truck braked in front of the door. Then she was actually inside the store, her feet stuck to the floor as Stephanie moved easily across it.

I can't leave her alone in here, thought Bett. *Look at that guy over there.* She couldn't quite place him, but he was familiar-looking and as sketch as sketch could be.

"Come on, Steph," she said, grabbing a soda for her friend and then Stephanie herself by the elbow. "Let's get out of here."

"Wait," said Stephanie. "I want to get some lip gloss, too."

"From here?" hissed Bett. The sketch guy moved up to the counter with two six-packs of beer.

"Yes, from here," Stephanie said. "Given that here is where we are." And she went over into the ancient cabinet that held tampons and pain relievers and, on the bottom shelf, a selection of lip glosses that were so dusty they looked like they had been sitting there since before Stephanie and Bett had ever even been alive.

"Stephanie, gross," said Bett.

"Don't you talk me out of it, you spineless crow," said Stephanie. "Who knows? Maybe they work better with age."

"Or maybe they melt your lips off," said Bett. She had her eye on the sketch guy, just in case. The door to the store banged open and a little girl about six years old came in and ran up to him.

"Daddy!" cried the little girl. "You came!"

"Sure did, honey munchkin," said the guy, glancing at Bett. "Pick what you want for a snack."

"A cider doughnut," said the little girl immediately.

"One cider doughnut for my little lady," said the sketch guy to the girl behind the counter, "and twelve liquid dreams for me."

The girl behind the counter laughed a little. "Okay, sir."

"I'm getting the Passion Petal," said Stephanie from her crouch over the lip glosses.

"I'll be ready to call 911 when you use it," Bett said back, her eyes still on the man.

He took up his paper bag. "All right, here we go!"

Bett panicked. Should she call her mom and tell her that a man who was clearly a drunk was going to get in his truck and drive with a little girl who was armed only with a cider doughnut? Maybe she could call her own dad, and he could call her mom. Bett knew she was being a candyass, but she didn't want to face her mother's anger over her not getting permission to get off the bus at Stephanie's house in the first place.

But before she could decide, Stephanie had *her* by the elbow and they were at the counter themselves, beside the jar of beef jerky sticks and the lottery tickets in their plastic case, Stephanie holding the soda now along with her little jar of ancient lip gloss and the man and the girl already out the flapping door and gone, only the icy outdoor air proof that they'd been inside the store at all.

I should have called, thought Bett as Stephanie paid cheerfully and led them out of the store.

When they went back inside at Stephanie's, her older brother, Bill, clattered down the stairs from the second floor and stopped short when he saw the bag in Stephanie's hand. Bill was three years older than Stephanie, a senior, who drove himself to school but refused to drive Stephanie because "no one drives around with a little sister," as Stephanie had reported him saying. Seeing him now, up close, he seemed almost like a man to Bett. It was clear he had to shave sometimes and everything.

"You did not go into Fancy Jim's," Bill said to his sister. "As dumb as even you are, you did not go in there."

"As dumb as even you are, you don't see that the 'Fancy Jim's' written on my bag means yes, I did go in there?"

"Who was in there?" asked Bill. "Who?"

"Relax," said Stephanie. "It was me, Bett here"—Bill tipped his chin up to Bett, who gave him a little wave, which she was immediately embarrassed about—"the counter girl, and some guy and his daughter."

"Was the guy kind of long-haired and super tan? Was he in a blue pickup?"

"I don't know about the pickup," said Stephanie, "but yeah about the hair, I guess."

"He had a blue pickup," said Bett. "Commercial plates." Both Stephanie and Bill looked at her in surprise. "What? My mom's a cop."

"She's a *cop*?" asked Bill, and immediately geeked. "Are you kidding me? Can I go in the cop car sometime? I want to do a ride along!"

"Probably not," Bett admitted. "But my mom always says that ninety-five percent of the work is service calls anyway. Not, like, murders."

"What do you mean, 'service calls'?" asked Bill. Bett saw that Stephanie was taking advantage of the conversation to sneak the soda out of her little bag.

"Like, helping old people. Getting people to go to the hospital when they need it. That kind of thing. They only investigate crimes pretty rarely."

"Now, *she*," said Bill, jabbing his finger toward Bett and addressing his sister, "is the kind of friend who's good to have around. She's got good stories, and better taste than you." He turned to Bett. "*You* didn't get a soda in that botulism pit, did you?" Bett shook her head. "Well, you both had a near escape. That motherflicking guy with the hair is bad news."

"I have to call my mom," Bett said abruptly. Both Bill and Stephanie looked surprised. "He stunk like alcohol and was about to drive with his daughter in the truck."

"Oh," said Bill. "Well. He only lives just up from us about a hundred yards. I think we would have heard a crash by now. I think you're off the hook."

Bett didn't know what to say. She didn't all the way agree about the off-the-hook thing. Should she call? But, once again, she'd get into a whole thing about not having gotten permission to get off at Stephanie's, and then there would be grounding and Bett spent enough time grounded as it was, getting in trouble for running inside at school.

Bill picked up Stephanie's Fancy Jim's bag as she drank down her entire Coke in one steady stream of gulps, eyes on her brother the whole time. Bill made to crumple the bag but stopped when his hand encountered the little jar of Passion Petal lip gloss. "Oh, hell no," he said. "You did not get lipstick there."

"It's lip *gloss*, idiot, and yes, I did."

"So not only did you want to poison your insides with a Fancy Jim soda, but you wanted to complete the job by making sure your lips would dissolve with toxic shit, too?"

"Shut up, Bill," said Stephanie, taking a hopeless slice at the bag. But Bill was already running outside, and they ran after him, still in their boots but coats unzipped, Stephanie belching all the way as the ancient soda sloshed around in her stomach.

"'Scuse me," she said, but they were still running after Bill, who was headed down one of the icy Christmas tree fields studded with the stumps of last month's cut-down trees to the bottom of a rocky hill, so Bett couldn't answer Stephanie to tell her she was excused.

Bett's long legs let her catch up with Bill fairly quickly, but not before he took the lip gloss out of the bag and hurled it as far as he could up the steep hill at the edge of the field. It landed, not on the hill itself, but on a ledge formed by a rocky outcropping about a third of the way up.

By the time Stephanie caught up with them, she was teary with rage and frustration.

"That was my *money*," she said. "MY MONEY! You don't get to pick what I do with my own cash, jerk!"

"You were going to poison yourself," said Bill.

Bett pretended to study the tree stumps around her. There were wet snuffles to her left.

Bill sighed. "Fine. I'll try and get your dumb lip balm," he said.

"Gloss," said Stephanie.

Bill rolled his eyes. "Gloss. But quit doing stupid shit."

Stephanie opened her mouth to retort, but, clearly realizing that Bill was about to risk his life for her lip gloss by climbing that ledge, she forbore as the three of them climbed over the fence and approached the steep foot of the hill.

Bill scrabbled up the hill to the bottom of the ledge and stood still a minute, looking at the icy rocky outcrop. He scratched at his head as he tried to figure out a way to get up to its top.

"Steph, I can't do it. There isn't any purchase!" he called down at last through cupped hands.

"There certainly was a purchase. I purchased that lip gloss with my own money and I expect you to pay me back!" Stephanie yelled back.

Bett, meanwhile, had been moving around the hill and

studied it and the ledge from the other side. Stephanie followed her while Bill shouted back from above.

"I mean 'purchase' like a grip, Brain." Bill clutched his hair, making it look as Einstein-y as the picture in the ninth-grade science lab. Then he turned and half walked, half skidded back down the hill and around to Bett and Stephanie. "I'll pay you your stupid money back. But by rights, I want it known that I saved your life from some debilitating disease by preventing you from putting that crap on your lips."

"I got this," said Bett.

"Thank you, Bett," said Bill. "Some people here don't seem to understand that I just was trying to save their life."

"No," said Bett. "I mean I can get up that ledge."

"Bett, I basically just saved my own life as well as my sister's by not being able to get up to that ledge. You just can't. There's no grip."

"Not on the face you were at," said Bett, walking up the hill. "But on this side."

Bill and Stephanie trailed behind Bett as she began to walk steadily up the steep hill.

"Bett, don't bother!" Stephanie said. "I can live without the sweet taste of Mr. Fancy Jim."

But the notion of climbing that ledge, slick with ice and snow, had become a compulsion now, and there was no way Bett wasn't going for it. Besides, Bett was eager to see an actual Fancy Jim product. She imagined a thick brown crust along the rim of the small jar, or maybe contents that had hardened like stone.

"Listen," said Bill, catching up with Bett once more, "it's not as easy as it looks. You can't tell from this angle, but that ledge is its own thing—there's this big gap between it and the actual hill."

Bett nodded. "I got it," she said again. And she moved purposefully toward the underhanging part of the rocky ledge.

"Bett, stop," said Stephanie. "It's just a crap lip gloss. Bill can't climb that ledge, and he's way older and taller than us."

"Taller than you. Not me." Bett had reached the littoral of hill and ledge and stood with her heart beating so hard it threatened to jump out of her chest and climb that ledge before Bett made it up there herself.

And then she was already climbing, finding handholds and using her feet as ballast against her own weight. *Oh my God, this is even better than running to school with four backpacks.* Every piece of the stone was clear to Bett, and she knew where to reach almost before she had to think about it. The hardest part was coming up, though. The chunk of rock below the lip of the ledge was almost as thick as Bett was tall, and she had no idea how she was going to get past that.

She looked up and saw the tiniest of handholds up and to the left. There was another one, a better one, higher up to the right. Could she do it? Could she use the small hand-hold long enough to swing her body up to the side and get to the good one? Her mother would never forgive her if she found out about this because Bett fell.

There's no way, said her brain. *You will never get up on that ledge.*

Oh, I will get up on that ledge, asswipe, Bett told her brain, and she swung her body to the left hard, then swung harder and faster than a pendulum and caught that right-hand handhold and then she was up and over on the ledge like an eagle landing on its aerie. And there was the little jar of sad-looking lip gloss, practically right in the middle of the icy stone.

"BETT!" Stephanie screamed. "WHAT THE HELL?"

"Got it." Bett called down and held up the lip gloss. "Catch." And she threw it down to Stephanie, who did not catch it but watched it tumble down past her. Bill skidded down the hill and picked it up.

The way back was much faster than the way up. Bett went between the ledge and the hill this time, which was a better way to come down, and then used the handholds she knew from the way up on the last part.

Stephanie's face was white when Bett reached her and Bill.

"Are you okay? Stephanie. What's wrong?"

"What's wrong? What's WRONG? Only that I just saw my best friend climb practically to her death up to that ledge. I was terrified to even tell you to get down! I was scared that even my voice would be enough to startle you and make you fall! Bett, how dumb *are* you?"

"Jesus," said Bett. "All I did was climb a stupid rock. I could show you. Come on. How sure-footed are you?"

"I am about one-tenth as sure-footed as you. Like, if we were rating people for sure-footedness and you were worth five Bettfuls of sure-footedness, I am at about half a Bett."

"More like one hundredth of a Bett," said Bill. "Bett, that was a climb for the ages. You are badass! You—"

But even as Stephanie and Bill were speaking, Bett could scarcely hear them for the joy that was pulsing through her. This was the best thing she had ever experienced in her entire life. She felt every second of the climb itself seared into her brain, every fear, every triumph of will. She had been given a glimpse inside a millisecond, inside forever.

"You scared the SHIT out of me, Bett!" Stephanie was done arguing about how many Bettworths of sure-footedness she had versus her brother.

"I'm sorry," Bett said helplessly. "I just wanted to help you." Which was true. Partly. "I knew I wouldn't fall."

"*I* didn't!"

"Well, I did. I live for stuff like that."

"Like what? Scaring the hell out of people?"

N. GRIFFIN

"No." But Bett couldn't find words for it that fit. "I just like, you know, physical challenges."

"Well, that was not just a physical challenge," Bill said. "That was, like, a physical *feat*."

"*Fizzicle feet.*" Stephanie couldn't help herself. "An ancient treat in the Fancy Jim's freezer. Popsicles made out of old unsold sodas—"

"—molded in the shape of feet?" finished Bett.

And both of them were shrieking with laughter again.

"This is where I leave you," said Bill. "This is a little too treble for my manhood."

Stephanie and Bett meandered behind Bill as he picked his way back down the hill toward the house, Bett herself still feeling pretty fizzicle—like her very blood was carbonated. She knew she could never live without more Fizzicle Feets, ever, not for the rest of her life. Mere backpack running, goal scoring, and home-run hitting were nothing compared to this.

When they had reached and climbed back over the fence, Bett took the little jar of lip gloss from Stephanie and turned the lid. There was the expected gritty scrape, and it was open. "Here's *your* Fizzicle Feet, Steph. Your reward, too, for not dying of fright while I was climbing the ledge." She extended the jar to Stephanie. "May you be the first to receive the kiss of Fancy Jim."

Stephanie shook her head. "I insist it be you, dumbass."

Their screams of laughter turned quiet, as they always

did, as they laughed so hard no sound came out and their cheeks were streaked with tears.

"I'm so glad you're feeling so happy."

Bett swung around. *What?*

And there was Bett's mom, in uniform. Bett was mortified. Stephanie looked terrified. All laughter ceased.

"Fingers broken?" Bett's mother asked as she led the girls back toward Stephanie's house, where she had parked her police car. "Some people have no fingers and yet *still* manage to place calls or text on their cell phones to let their parents know where they are. With their noses, I've even heard. Which may be the way you get to use your phone after you get it back in two weeks, my girl." She extended her hand, and Bett, unquestioning, gave her mother her phone.

"How did you know I was here?" she asked once she had said a weird, shamefaced good-bye to Stephanie, and she and her mother were in the car.

"Bett, I am a cop. I know how to find a kid. I'm not letting you in on all my techniques at this moment. Not exactly seeing you like a buddy on a ride-along with me right now."

"Whatever," said Bett.

Her mother applied the brakes. She turned to Bett. "Would you like to say that again?" she asked.

"Mom, what if someone pulls up behind us and needs to go forward?" said Bett.

"I will direct them to go around my vehicle," said her mother. "Well?"

"No," said Bett. "I would not like to say that again."

"Excellent," said her mother, and home they went.

Bett should have called her dad.

10

Thursday, Eleventh Grade, Off the Bus

SOMEHOW DRIVING THROUGH CIVILIZATION ON THE bus and arriving back at this slope that led up and home made Bett feel more than ever like the little house her mother had built for them was more shack than house. It wasn't like her mother had even known how to build a house before about six months ago. She just got a bunch of library books about building one during Bett's sophomore year and did it, starting in the spring and finishing it up right at the end of summer so they could move in before school started.

Her mother was like that. Like Bett. Strong as a tank and very pragmatic, good at figuring out how things worked. Bett had worked on the house, too, until it felt too good, too Plus, but her mother's solid competence made even that work mostly unnecessary. By the time summer came to an end all that was left for Bett to do was help with the insulation, which didn't involve fat rolls of cotton-candy-looking stuff or spray foam as she'd expected, but books. It turned out that you could insulate a house with them. Bett's mother had read about it. So they used all their own and ones they found on free tables at yard sales and boxes of books people sold for a dollar at the thrift store.

"You know," said her mother when they were done lining the walls, "I like the look of that. All those books. I think I'll leave it and we can skip the drywall." Which was the one thing Bett had been looking forward to, because she enjoyed drywalling, actually. But it was just as well. Even drywalling would probably count as too Plus. And Bett knew her mother was just glad to be done and able to get out of the house they had lived in after Bett's father had left them.

"Two years is a long time in a house you hate," said her mother. Bett was glad to leave, too. It wasn't like she was dying to see her father, ever, anyway, much less stay in the house they had all shared.

Whatever. The new SIM card house looked weird, like a tiny crammed library, like Bett and her mother both read more than they really did. The racket of all those spines and titles jarred Bett's nerves, and the books themselves, smelling like dust and mildew, didn't make her feel like she was supposed to read or think much. The opposite, actually. It made it look like thinking was pretty well taken care of already, so Bett didn't have to bother. So it was at once too noisy and a relief.

Now, following the row of trees that lined the skinny path along the river edge to the right of the SIM card house, Bett pelted up the slope, away from Eddie, even though she knew she'd have to do something drastic later to undo the good feeling of this Plus run. To her left the river ran fast and focused toward the bay, its banks scrabbled with tough green-brown plants that stuck out, stubby and spare, over the rushing water and stones beneath. The river noise was just like the loud, ambient, chittery noise at the school, and exactly what Bett needed now. Numbed-out left ear and no thinking about the day. She ground the soles of her sneakers into the dirt and stopped short when she crested the slope above the river, breathing hard but completely still at last. Crows flew up from the river and landed on the path in front of Bett, craaking and arguing and making a din that only helped Bett not hear.

There was a man in the water. He was a distance away but Bett could see him clearly, tall and brown in the foaming rapids. She couldn't see his face, but his curly dark hair shook as he drew both arms across his chest and over one shoulder, like an old-time athlete cheering for himself. But no; he threw both arms up and in front of him and there was a glint of something arching over the gray of the water. From here it weirdly looked like a piece of the man's own shoulder. Then Bett got it. *He's fishing. What for?* she wondered. She hadn't really thought about what fish lived down there in the river. Angling had never been one of her things. But it made sense that there were fish, and Bett knew cool weather was good for fishing.

The man must have sensed her looking because he turned his face up to her and lifted his arm in a wave. Should Bett wave back? She bet he was the neighbor her mother talked about. Or what passed for a neighbor here. Her mother had built their new little house at the tip of a strip of land all by itself so there wasn't any true "next door" like in town. Or "neighbors." Well, there must be neighbors, because Bett knew that when her mother built their teeny house herself with her own two hands, the closest other person to their house lent her some kind of saw. So there were people here, but not many, and not exactly near.

The man was still looking at her. He called something she couldn't make out with her filled, numb ear.

"What?" she called back.

The man waved again. Bett wondered if he wanted her to pick her way to the water below, if it would be rude if she didn't because he was their new neighbor or if maybe it would be stupid because she wasn't so idiotic that she was going to talk to some man hanging out in a river in case he turned out to be a perv. Besides, she never went down to the river—not anymore. Though she couldn't help seeing it, since it was everywhere in this town.

The sun peeked out wanly from behind the pale gray expanse of sky overhead, and the man was smiling. The river was rough and fast, slate gray with little caps of white in places like hot milk.

"Hello," called Bett from where she was, as sort of a compromise, standing with her hand over her opposite wrist.

"Hi," called the man back, and smiled at her again. His eyes looked very dark from here. He was wearing an enormous pair of pants held up by suspenders. The pants were gunmetal gray and shone wetly in the water. What were those kind of pants called again? Bett couldn't remember.

The man followed her eyes and glanced down at his pants. He said something.

"What?" she asked.

The man repeated himself, but even though she was watching him closely she didn't catch his words, what with the added racket of the river.

He shouted again.

"Whalers?" guessed Bett and he nodded. "Oh." Was it possible there were actual whales in Salt River? That seemed insane, even if Salt River was called that because it was just that, a saltwater river. But it wasn't deep enough for an actual whale.

He said something else, about being her new neighbor,

probably, introducing himself, but Bett's attention was caught by the movement of his whalers as he shifted position in the rushing water to talk to her. The pants moved silently through the water, quiet and big and slow. The name made sense. Bett imagined the big, loose pants squeaking against the rocks underwater, crying like whale song.

The man watched her and threw the line again.

"I'm Bett," she hollered suddenly. "You met my mother? She built our house."

"Yes," the man shouted back, his words suddenly clear. "I know you're Bett. And your mother worked very hard on your house."

He seemed lovely, his smile very kind. Bett closed her eyes against the cold gray air and the smell of the water was everywhere.

The man in the water spoke again. Bett frowned. He repeated himself, but she still couldn't make out what he was saying.

Bett stood on one foot. Then she shook her head and backed away. Back to the path, and then she ran Plusly and wrongly again, skidding and tripping over rocks and sand to the tiny shack of a house she lived in now.

At the house there was much more wind than on the path. There always was. There was nothing to break its force. The trees ended here, and there were only grasses, sharp and green, and the skinny strip of dirt that led up to the house. All through the first days of the summer when Bett's mother had brought her over to look at the progress she'd made on the little house, Bett's legs were full of tiny slices from those grasses.

"Wear jeans," her mother had said, but Bett was committed to the short-jean-shorts mortification, and the grass slices were another good antidote to any accidental Pluses that might come up during the course of a day, too. And it wasn't like their house overlooked real, warm-weather kind of water anyway, with sand and sunshine and people in bathing suits. It was just a rocky semi-bay near the mouth of a river, its water scraggly and cold even in July, Bett knew, although she wouldn't let herself go near enough to touch it, not even to drabble a finger through its surface. The river itself was too Plus.

She slowed to a walk as she reached the stretch of path just in back of the house.

"Mom," she called, crashing through the door. "Mom!"

"What?" said her mother. She was right there. Actually, she was in the kitchen, but the house was so small, all she needed to do was back up one step and poke her head into the living room, where the doorway framed the pale light in which Bett was standing. "Bett, you are a pile of dirt. Please remember to bang your feet before you come in!"

"What?" said Bett.

"Bang your feet!"

Bett banged them.

"Not in here! Bett, for God's sake. Use your head."

"Whatever," said Bett. At least her left ear was unplugging a bit. She bent down and used the side of her hand to force her foot dirt into a pile and pushed as much as she could into the palm of the other hand.

"A broom would be better," said her mother. "But I appreciate the gesture. How was the first day?"

"Do you have any whalers?" Bett asked in response.

"What?" Her mother's brow crinkled.

"Whalers," said Bett. She thought it would be kind of cool for her mother to be able to walk right into the river, like the man had, not getting wet. Maybe she could even walk straight across to the other side. She imagined the weight of the water pushing against her mother's body and the work of walking through it against a strong, sure current.

"You mean people who hunt whales?" her mother asked. "What, you want roommates in here? Please. It was all I could do to build a house big enough for the two of us."

"Come *on*." Bett exhaled with disgust. "Not people. Like, those big gray clown pants."

Her mother stared at her. "Bett," she said. "Help me."

"I met a man. The neighbor man with the saw, I think. He was standing in the water with clown pant things on."

"Clown pants!" her mother exclaimed. "Bett, I don't think that was the neighbor man. And that guy with the saw wasn't an actual neighbor, just someone who lives on the way back to town."

"Well, this man seemed really nice," said Bett. "And he knew you." *He knew me, too.* But she didn't say that part out loud.

"Bett. What the hell? It's not enough that I've been a cop for twenty years and you've sat through more child-defense programs than any kid in the USA? You *still* talk to strangers? Jesus holy God, what am I going to—"

"I didn't talk to him *much*," said Bett. "I backed away. But it was just the saw guy, I'm pretty sure. He looked familiar. I knew you'd be mad."

"Well, Bett," said her mother, "you are correct there. I have to tell you that the man who lent me the saw is really not the type to wear clown pants to stand in the middle of a river. I think who you saw is probably a crazy person, and you did the right thing by backing away from him."

"I *know*," said Bett. "But he didn't seem crazy. And he needed those pants. He would have gotten wet otherwise." She stood up, holding her little handful of dirt carefully so it didn't spill back onto the floor. "They were, like, water-proofed or rubberized or something."

There was a little silence. Then: *"Waders,"* said her mother. *"Waders.* I think what you mean is waders."

Waders. *Waders.* Of course. Deep gray sea shapes stretched away and high-pitched song sounds faded into nothing but something sturdy and practical. Of course, waders. Bett remembered the word for them now. What was all that about the whale song? Not a very Bett-like thought.

Something, though. Something.

The man greeting her, his eyes so kind. Bett couldn't shake the feeling that she shouldn't have backed away.

"Are you sure you heard him correctly?" Bett's mother asked, peering into Bett's face like an overweening cat.

"Mom, my ear is fine." Which was actually true right then, but Bett wasn't about to tell her about the ear go-outs of the day and discuss the reasons for them. The principal had already taken care of that. And even though the thought of her mother all up in school business was a giant ugh, if she was honest, Bett was still feeling uneasy about those fiery, burning pictures, and wouldn't mind if her mother got to the bottom of who did it after all.

Still, Bett and her mom had fought about her ear so many times, Bett wished she could rip it off and present it to the woman. But the upside was that Bett knew she could nearly always get off the hook of hearing her mother by turning away from her face. Even if she could still actually hear, which she really pretty much always could because her right ear was fine, it was convenient to make her mother, and teachers, and anyone, especially her father— who she refused to see and barely spoke to on the phone, even though he called and e-mailed and texted all the time, living in the next town with his Floozy, as her mother and Aunt Jeanette referred to her—think that she could not.

"You wouldn't tell me if you couldn't hear, anyway," said her mother, and Bett said nothing.

Just as well that there were no waders in the house. Bett might have been too tempted to do the work of water-walking herself.

That reminded her of the satisfaction of pounding up the slope from the bus, a true Plus that Bett knew had to be undone—now. The familiar terror and anxiety mounted in her stomach until she couldn't take it, until all she wanted was to grab a bag of Oreos and run up the four little steps into the even smaller SIM card space that was her room and hunch over her sneaker sole to eat the cookies and retrace the STOP printed there until the ink was as black as it had been when she wrote it this morning.

But her mother was already talking to her again.

"What's all this about art being destroyed up at the school?" she asked Bett.

Bett shrugged quickly. "I don't know," she said. "Some deranged person. You all will catch them."

"We'll do our damnedest," said her mother. "I don't like the thought of you in that school with someone like that on the loose."

"Quit being a cop at me."

"I'm not," said her mother simply. "I'm being a mother."

"I'll be fine," said Bett.

Her mother raised her eyebrows briefly and turned back to the stove and, fast as a catamount, Bett grabbed the bag of Oreos from the cupboard and ran up to her room and ate and ate and ate, hoping the carbs and sugar would still the well of terror in her mind, but also knowing that terror would be replaced by self-hate for eating too much, a loathing for the big body the Oreos helped make, and that was not better than the terror. But it would cancel out the school anxiety and the running Plus, and that was what Bett was after.

The sugar finally hit her body like a ton of bricks and Bett lay on her bed, eyes closed, beached like a whale and almost asleep. Thoughts of the day floated unbidden through her mind. Ranger, the smoke, the flames, this new bus. It was so weird that Eddie the bus driver also worked at the Vet Social Service Center with her dad. Bett didn't like it one tired bit. She wanted her worlds separate, and Eddie intersecting with her father was as creepy and unwelcome as the psycho art slasher-burner at the school.

Bett shook her head slowly as her ear filled again and went out. Her father and his life were the last things she wanted to think about right now.

11

TWO YEARS AGO . . . In the spring of
ninth grade, the ice was cracked in the ragged ribbon of the
river and so was the Venn diagram between Stephanie's
friends and Bett's. Now instead of the intersection of the
circles being filled with just her and Stephanie, the two of
them hung out with groups of one or the other's friends as
well, planned or not, and, despite her mother's annoyance
at that first impromptu visit to Stephanie's, Bett now had
standing permission to get off the bus there whenever she
wanted.

Stephanie's parents were divorced. Her father lived in
Rayfen, just the next town over, and her mother, small and
redheaded with slim, pale fingers, worked at the insurance
office here in Salt River. Stephanie's two uncles and Bill

worked the Christmas tree farm, the work more intense in season and lighter the rest of the time, planting and maintaining the trees.

Mrs. Roan wasn't often home when Stephanie and Bett got off the bus together. When she did come home after work, though, Bett noticed, if she was still there, that Mrs. Roan often had a bouquet of flowers in her arms, all made up with ribbons and bows.

"I always tell them to gift wrap," she told the girls. "Why not? It's nice to feel like you got a present. Like a Happy Birthday to Me."

"Let me unwrap them," Stephanie begged, and her mother always let her before she trimmed the stems and arranged them in vases herself with those slim fingers, her movements so delicate that they made Bett shudder and want to grab the flowers from her and just shove them in the vase already.

Stephanie's mother called Bett's house once and asked to speak to Bett's dad.

"Insurance policy," she told Bett. But her dad wasn't home.

"I like that Stephanie," said Bett's mother. "She's got a way about her. You know what it is? Charisma, that's what. That is a kid who has a lot of charisma."

"Like myself," said Bett's Aunt Jeanette, who was over, as she always was, Led Zeppelin playing on the stereo again, and Bett wanting to die because not only was

Aunt Jeanette so sure she was charismatic, but her neck was working in an awful, chicken-like way in time to the music, and Bett's mother's neck was doing the same, and it was all so painful to witness that Bett had to leave the room.

At any rate, Bett's and Stephanie's friends had mixed a little, albeit not smooth like a cake, but lumpy like a fruit cobbler. Still, they were mixing, and making out was a thing now, which did its bit to bring the groups together. Fresh blood was always a good thing. Stephanie was nearly always one of the ones making out, most memorably at the last accidental gathering of kids at Stephanie's own house. They were all downstairs in the basement, Stephanie sitting on the washing machine kissing a boy who was perched on the dryer, while another boy was crouched on the other side of the washing machine, kind of making out with Stephanie's arm. Sometimes Bett made out, too, often with this random boy from the Catholic school who admired her muscles and long legs.

Bett was impressed at how Stephanie was almost universally liked. Not just for making out, but as a friend, too. *How does she do it?* wondered Bett, but she knew. Sure, Stephanie was pretty, but she was also funny and liked everybody. Plenty of people liked Bett, too, but there seemed to be some social secret to people that Stephanie just knew how to access, whereas what Bett just knew was how to memorize a license plate at a glance and catch a foul ball. Bett knew she was her mother's daughter, competent and strong, someone who could help move a couch. This generally made her feel powerful and tough, but sometimes, if Stephanie was making out with someone and there was no one readily nearby to talk to, Bett wondered if maybe it would have been good to have inherited some of her dad's more delicate genes after all, though he was so skinny anyone could snap him like a twig.

Stephanie disagreed about Bett's dad's looks. "Your dad is good-looking," she said, "for a dad."

"Ugh!" shouted Bett. "Don't say stuff like that about people's dads!"

But opinions about fathers notwithstanding, Stephanie was generous with sharing boy secrets and makeup tips with Bett. Stephanie wanted to do makeup tutorials online someday so she watched a lot of them now and then practiced what she learned on Bett on the bus whenever it stopped, the application punctuating the trip to school like ellipses. Stephanie would get in trouble at her school for so much makeup, but not Bett, who had grown to kind of love the way Stephanie made her look, not like a Twinkler but like something even better. And by now, with the crocuses coming up and it being actual genuine spring, although still pretty cold out, Stephanie had made Bett up so many times that Bett could do it herself at home if it was just her dad around in the mornings.

"You look great, honey!" he always said, and Bett felt

guilty for thinking him too skinny and too *whatever-you-want*. "Like a bird with sleek, beautiful plumage."

But if Bett's mom was the one who was still around in the morning, makeup was strictly a bus thing, done between stops and jounces, because Bett's mother believed in no makeup to school before you were fifteen, never mind plumage, and so Bett had to make sure it was washed off before she went home, too.

"You're actually really good at this," said Stephanie one morning when Bett was the one making her own self up. "I think you're, like, my protégé."

The two of them were especially excited this morning because Bett was going to sleep over at Stephanie's after school, even though it was a school night, and Bett had a Fizzicle Feet in mind that was so good she couldn't think of anything else.

Fizzicle Feets completely were a Thing now. Usually Bett begged Stephanie to think of them. "Give me one," she begged, at her house or Steph's, and Stephanie always began with guilty hemming and hawing about not wanting Bett to get hurt and offering the stupidest easiest things, like jumping off the picnic table, for God's sake, with Bett pleading for something harder and harder and harder until they finally came up with something. If he was home, Bill often came to watch, too, and helped think of some of the best ones.

Thus, so far, Fizzicle Feets had included:

1) Bett jumping from that rocky ledge at Stephanie's house to the hill it abutted. ("It's like an eight-foot leap. With a running start!" Bett told Stephanie that day, and showed her on the ground first how easy it was. "Your mother will arrest me for killing you!" Stephanie worried, but Bett said no, she'd just finish killing Bett herself first.)

2) Climbing up to the top of the roof of Stephanie's house. Stephanie leaned against the first gas pump and watched as Bett scaled the porch roof—easy with a run and a jump to grab the lip of that porch roof, which was flat, and then all she had to do was swing over onto it, walk across, and then climb up the steep eaves to the tip of the housetop itself. It was so easy, it was barely a Fizzicle Feet, so Bett wanted to jump down from the eaves part as well. But Stephanie had cried actual tears of worried fury, so Bett didn't.

3) This was a good one: letting herself be chased, through appreciable and foot-pulling mud, through the one Christmas tree field where they were not, repeat, not allowed to go, because there was a pack of coyotes living up in that field right now, and one of the males was not happy at all to see Bett in his space. Thank God for her speed and her strong legs. The feeling of legging it up and over that fence with the coyote snarling and howling in the field behind her was worth it. Worth it. More than. Because breathing

hard and muscles spent and being one inch from danger was the everything of it all.

But the best Fizzicle Feet was going to be today. It was one Bett had thought of, because Stephanie never would have, not in the least because it involved using her brother's mountain bike without really letting him know, which how could they right now, anyway, because he was staying late at the Catholic school to rehearse for some performance or other—maybe the band with his French disgusting horn, with its spit valve that Bett didn't even want to hear about, much less have demonstrated to her.

Anyway, this Fizzicle Feet was going to be done at night, after midnight even, and Bett wouldn't tell Stephanie what it was, except for the Bill bike part, and Stephanie was part scared and part excited and hugely afraid, as she always was.

"It's tough to witness you almost die on, like, a weekly basis," she said to Bett as they lay in the twin beds in Stephanie's room, waiting for the house to quiet. Bett had already written Flight on the sole of her shoe five days ago, and had been jogging it into herself ever since.

"I never almost die, Steph," Bett objected.

"It looks like you do."

But Bett couldn't find the words to say that a Fizzicle Feet was so far the opposite of almost dying, there wasn't even a word for it.

Finally, the house was silent and the girls crept outside and into the small side barn where Bill's bike was.

"Going for a ride?"

It was Bill himself, and both girls jumped a mile, hearts pounding.

Stephanie socked him. "What is wrong with you?" she whisper-yelled, not wanting to wake up their mother.

"What is wrong with *you*?" Bill whisper-yelled back. "Are you out here meeting some guy? Because, Stephanie, there really are some sketch dudes out there and—"

"No," Bett interrupted. "It's me. I was going to use your bike. Not for a guy. Fizzicle Feet."

Bill's face, weird in the silver of the moonlight, changed on a dime.

"What is it?" he whispered eagerly.

"She won't tell," said Stephanie, her gray hair ribbon straggling down her back.

"I will now, since I guess I really should ask you before I take your bike," said Bett.

"Thoughtful of you," said Bill. "Spill."

"Well," said Bett. "You know that ravine under the rock ledge that goes to the river?"

"You mean where that path cuts into the slope?"

"Yeah," said Bett. "I'm going to ride down it. On your bike. Mine's just a road bike, and I thought yours would be, you know, heftier."

"He won't let you," said Stephanie immediately. "Bill, don't let her! Don't! She'll kill herself, all the rocks on that path! Bett," she pleaded, "please no. Come on. This is the stupidest one you've ever thought of."

"If by 'stupid' you mean 'badass,'" said Bill, "I am going to let you borrow the shit out of my bike, Bett, and then I am going to video you with my phone with the night vision app on, and then we'll post it to YouTube, where you will become the most famous badass ever."

"Bill!" But Stephanie was ignored and Bill gallantly pushed the bike up the hill to the lip of the ravine and the rocky path. Bett's heart was already pounding with the love-hate of the Feet, Stephanie nearly weeping behind her.

"Bett, I am not kidding. That is no path. That is a vertical DROP, Bett! Bett, you will die."

"Shut up, please," said Bett. She had the handlebars in her hands now, one foot on a pedal, the other on the ground.

"Bett—"

"Shut up, Steph," said Bill, holding out his phone to frame Bett in its lens. "Damn. I want to watch it in, like, real life. Stephanie, will you video it?"

"No!"

"Shut up!" both Bill and Bett hissed.

"Fine," said Bill. "I'll do it myself. Bett, just go when you're ready. I'm all set."

"I will." Bett looked down at the path, the big boulder about halfway down, the silver-tipped current swirling below.

NOW. And she was rocketing down, bumping from

stone to stone, bike leaping and landing and leaping again until Bett reached that big rock and YES—she was flying, bike in her hands, feet still on the pedals, and there was the moment, the moment inside the split second, inside forever and no time at all. Then she was back on the ground, coasting down, braking but somehow winding up in the freezing river anyway.

"BADASS!" Bill was yelling and turning around and slapping his legs up at the lip of the ravine as Bett dripped out of the river, shivering, and made her way back up the slope with Bill's bike. She hoped the water hadn't wrecked it.

But Bill didn't seem to care about that at all. "BAD-EFFING-ASS!"

Bett knew it. She knew it and loved it and her blood was singing. She tucked in her smile and wheeled the bike the rest of the way up, which was slippy and took some doing.

When she got near the top, Stephanie was crying and Bill grabbed the bike from Bett and tugged it over the lip of the ravine. Then he dropped it and pulled Bett up, too, and slapped her on the shoulder before enveloping her in a hug.

"Steph, I am fine," said Bett when Bill released her. "I am *always* fine."

"No, you aren't!" said Stephanie. "You are *bleeding*!"

Bett looked where Stephanie pointed, at the confluence

of veins on the heel of her hand, blood seeping out of a tiny, deep cut.

"Must have been a rock in the water," said Bett. "Steph, I don't even feel it. Just needs a Band-Aid."

"Here," said Stephanie, still sniffling. And she pulled her gray, raggly edged ribbon off her head and handed it to Bett. "Press."

"Are you giving her a *dirty ribbon* to put on a wound?" asked Bill, repulsed, and Stephanie punched him.

"It's not dirty," she said. Then, still sniffling, she said, "Fine. Let's watch you on Bill's phone," and she and Bett started up with their laughing.

"Please shut up and don't make me regret coming out here," said Bill. He held his phone in front of them, and they watched the Fizzicle Feet together, Bett's heart leaping with the bike, soaring over the boulder in the path almost as it had when she'd done it. The three of them stood on the hill in the moonlight, shoulders close, watching Bett fly down the slope again and again.

Stephanie might be the one who was in the Catholic school, but Bett was the one who, in those milliseconds of what-if, saw the face of God.

12

Autumn, Eleventh Grade,
Two in the Early Morning of Friday

BETT SAT UP IN BED AND PULLED OUT HER PHONE.

YouTube. Play.

The doll Rayfenetta was making was coming out magnificently. The armor shone with its intertwined triangles, the wings were huge, and there was a helmet on the doll's beautiful head, with the real and fake hair braids tumbling out from beneath.

Bett picked and picked at the scar on her wrist.

"Like I said before," Rayfenetta said, "one of the best things about Blythe dolls is that you can change out the eyes. I don't like these green ones for this doll. Watch."

And she popped the eyes out.

Bett flinched.

"The more you do it, the easier it gets."

Rayfenetta took up one eye and switched it to another side—bright and almost silver.

"And see? See how that color makes the metal stand out?"

Bett did see.

But Rayfenetta didn't change out the other eye. Instead, she took the tiny flower she had made in the last video and stuck it in the other socket. Then she drew vines around it like a tattoo.

Bett picked her scar until it bled.

13

Still Around Two in the Horrible Morning

STILL NO SLEEP FOR BETT. PARTLY IT WAS BECAUSE OF the picture slasher-burner with all the teachers and principal and her mother clearly worried about the incident, too. But some of it was not because of any reason, particularly, just a restlessness that was familiar to her and for which there was often no cure. *Get up already*, she told herself, and, resigned to not sleeping, went down the narrow stairs to the kitchen and made herself a cup of tea. As long as she watched the teapot, she could stop it before it whistled and brought her mother down into the kitchen to see what Bett was up to.

But the tea, caffeinated, turned out to be a terrible idea, and the restlessness and anxiety grew. What could she do? A shower would wake up her mother, too, but Bett had washed her feet in warm water once this summer to bathe a cut from the grasses, and found it so soothing that she bathed them now sometimes on purpose when she couldn't sleep. So she went into the tiny bathroom lined with books and filled the sink with warm water and washed each foot, one at a time.

Bett looked at her feet. They were pretty, she had to admit, though she would never wear sandals and flip-flops to show them off like a Twinkler girl.

Bett thought for a minute.

I haven't in forever.

But her feet were so warm. Could she? Or would it be too Plus?

Hesitantly, Bett stuck her hand under the sink until she found her old basket of nail polishes, all of them more than two years old. She hadn't touched them since—since. But there they were.

Not red. Not pink. Not a color *color. Too Plus.*

From the basket, Bett plucked a small bottle of polish the color of hematite stones and went to work. The brush on her warm, lovely toes was calming, getting it just right, not going outside the edge of her toenails. There. Done. Warm, lovely feet, and now maybe she could rest, toes outside her blankets.

She still couldn't sleep, though. She just rested, looking at her feet and thinking about the man in the river. Her thoughts drifted and swayed until they landed, unwelcome, on her father. Bedtime with her father when she was young had been a mixed bag at best. He was always wanting to tell her stories about fairies and other little creatures with wings, and she used to have to put out her hand and tell him, "Stop. Tell me about real stuff."

One time the "real stuff" had been him telling her about vets. She had heard about what vets were from Career Day in kindergarten and was very excited to see what kind of animals her father worked with.

Maybe elephants. Or maybe whales and birds.

"Oh," her father had said. "You're thinking about 'vet' as a word that's short for 'veterinarian.' They're the ones who work with animals. I work with 'vet*erans*,' who are people who have gone to war for our country and come home again."

"What's war?" Bett had asked, and her father sighed and ran his hand through his hair.

"It's when two countries who can't get along fight," he said simply.

"You mean like punching?" asked Bett, wheeling her own fists around.

"Sort of," said her father. He looked very much like he wished they were still listening to his story about the beings with wings. "But worse. Sometimes they hurt each other so badly people die. Or come home hurt. On the outside or the inside."

"Oh," said Bett. She didn't really get it, but that was

okay. She wheeled her arms around in punches again.

"Your uncle was in the Gulf War," said her dad.

"Which uncle?"

"Your uncle Todd," said her father. "He died in that war before you were born." His eyes clouded. "I loved him very much." He went quiet. "He's why I work with vets now," he said at last.

"Vets, vets, vets," said Bett, bouncing where she sat in her bed. "Maybe one of them will let you ride a whale. Or pet a bird." Her father smiled, but his eyes were sad. Then he gave her a hug. It lasted too long, and Bett pulled away, impatient.

"Tell me a different story," Bett demanded. "One about something good. Like tractors."

"I'll tell you about four-wheelers. Your uncle Todd loved then."

"Did you love them, too?"

Her dad's eyes grew sad again. "No," he said. "Not my thing. But I think you'll like them, when you're older. You're a lot like your uncle. Built like him, too."

"I'm a lot like Mom, I thought you said."

"That you are. She reminds me of Todd, too. That's part of why I love you both so much." And her dad had kissed her forehead and then told her about Uncle Todd four-wheeling for the rest of that story time.

Stop. Stop thinking about him. That was ages ago, and you don't have to think about him anymore.

So Bett lay perfectly still, thinking of nothing until she just told herself it was officially time to get moving and get ready for the next day of eleventh grade. She got up and dressed with her hair in its messy pile on the top of her head, and a fresh pair of cut-up jean shorts over her butt. Yesterday only made wearing shorts again today more necessary. More mortification to enjoy, only *don't think about that*, because then the mortification would turn into a weird backward kind of Plus, and God knew how she'd deal with that.

As she put on her sneakers she thought, briefly, that it was a shame no one was going to see her pretty feet with her hematite toes, but she swallowed the thought with the Pop-Tarts she chose for breakfast and was out of the house and at the bottom of the slope easily fifteen minutes before the bus could be expected. She mentally slapped her own hand in a spectral high five that she had successfully avoided her mother, who went to the station house late on Fridays, and avoided her own brain as well, with which she had only upset irritation. Except for the idea about the toes. That had been an okay part, even if it verged on too Plus.

She was so tired, she couldn't pay attention to the morning chatter of the bus ride, even though Dan was clearly wanting to talk to the bus at large about the fire and the art destroyer, and Ranger was cakesing, and Mutt was pissed, and Eddie shouted at them periodically. Bett's inability to focus was actually relaxing, sort of like taking a nap with her eyes open.

But Eddie ruined it.

Bett was last off the bus, and when she'd landed on the sidewalk in front of the school, Eddie roared, "BETT!" and made her turn around and pay attention at last.

Eddie cleared his throat. "Bett," he said, "I need to talk to you."

What? What about? Some comment about her weight, probably, or some crap about talking with her father. Whichever it was, Bett wanted no truck with Eddie and talking. He could keep his thoughts about her weight to himself.

This was where pretended deafness was a blessing. Bett pelted toward the school. She didn't need to hear what Eddie had to say. Therefore, this running did not count as a Plus.

14

TWO YEARS AGO . . . Stephanie had
fallen asleep as soon as they came in from the Bike Ravine
Fizzicle Feet that ninth-grade night, falling into her bed as if
she were already dreaming. But not Bett. She was too electric, too alive, too everything. She lay in the twin bed next
to Stephanie's with the ribbon around her wrist and looked
out the window, reliving the night until it turned to day.

At six, she woke Stephanie up. "School," she said
simply.

"Ugh," moaned Stephanie.

"Get up," said Bett. "We have to show them we're
'responsible' if we ever want another school-night sleep-
over."

"I don't think I ever do, if it means waking up," moaned

Stephanie. But she sat up, her long, Twinkler-adjacent hair falling forward over her face. "Also if it means that's when you do the worst and most death-defying of your Fizzicle Feets."

Bett swallowed her smile. No denying it; last night was supreme and superb and there was no way she wasn't going to try to top it.

Ankle on the opposite knee, in tiny letters this time, she wrote Bill.

This morning there were even more buds on the trees than there had been the day before, more crocuses, more everything, although it was still freezing as they stood bouncing on their toes at the foot of Stephanie's porch, waiting for the school bus to chug up the hill before they headed to the bottom of the driveway to climb up the steep steps of the bus.

"You're psyched, aren't you?" said Stephanie. "You're psyched you went down that hill and flew over that rock. How? How can you do that and not feel out-of-your-mind scared?"

Bett shrugged. "How do you make everyone like you on the spot and know how to handle any boy just the right way?"

"I don't know," said Stephanie simply. "I just want people to be happy."

The bus didn't come and didn't come. It was so cold,

Bett worried that the crocuses would die and full-on spring wouldn't arrive at all, which did happen some years here— Salt River went straight from winter to summer in a week, it seemed, and spring pretty much got skipped.

Stephanie looked at her, head cocked. "I wish I were more like you," she said finally, just as Bett was starting to get weirded out.

"What? Are you kidding? You're pretty and popular and everyone likes you as soon as they meet you. You make everyone feel special."

"Shut up," said Stephanie. "I want to be tall and strong and athletic like you, and have boys as friends like you do and not just as maybe-make-out people, and I want to feel like I could figure out regular things easily like you."

"What do you mean?"

"Like how you and your mom figured out how to redo the drywall when the ceiling in your living room flooded that time."

Bett shrugged. "That was more common sense than anything else. We just read how and did it."

"But me and my mom never would."

"Well, me and my mom would never have the whole town think we should be models, either," said Bett.

"I want to feel as free as you do," said Stephanie. "As free to do what you want, when you want to do it. I love that about you, Bett."

"Even when you yell at me for doing Fizzicle Feets?"

Stephanie nodded. "Even then."

Down the hill, the diesel of the bus finally sounded through the cold morning air.

"Remember how you said that time that you wanted to be a bus driver when you were little?" Stephanie reminded Bett, who laughed.

"I did!" said Bett. "I thought it would be the best to drive a school bus."

"That is the cutest thing."

"Shut up," said Bett.

"You shut up," said Stephanie back. "Watch. I'm going to be like you for real. My first and only Fizzicle Feet." And she climbed up the five porch stairs of her house and threw her arms back as if to leap.

A five-year-old could do that, thought Bett, but she made sure her face looked anticipatory and interested as the bus came closer and Stephanie leaped from the top porch step. But her jump was

too much—

not enough—

Stephanie was going to fall and slam her head against the ground like a basketball—

Bett ran, to Stephanie, to the gas pumps, feeling her foot stomp on the nozzle hose, which was lying like a snake in the iced dirt of the driveway, and then there was a giant *CRACK*, ROAR—

and everything was everywhere: backpacks, shoes, Bett, Stephanie. Everything was everywhere in the burst of those pumps, so loud Bett heard nothing. Jagged with pain, she saw only Stephanie and flames, Stephanie lying at the bottom of the porch steps, one of her eyes bloody and oh God! all the blood all the heat flames all around.

A long time of screaming with no sounds. The bus stopped and the driver and kids all seemed to be screaming something, but they'd agreed not to make a sound, either, out of respect for Bett, she guessed? Fire people with hoses. Mrs. Roan tearing out of the house in not enough clothes. Ambulance. Cop car but not Bett's mom's, who was there in her flannel pajamas and coat, also screaming at Bett even though Bett couldn't hear a word. Bett searing with pain.

Where was Bett's dad? Over there, he was crouched over Stephanie, pushed away by the EMTs, Stephanie's mother with not enough on crouched over her daughter, too, weeping, but like everybody else, she'd decided not to do it with a sound.

Bett's mother grabbing a paper cup and a pen from the cop, writing *BETT CAN YOU HEAR ME?* on the cup, which was so hilarious because did her mom mean can you hear the words she'd just *written down* was Stephanie still by the gas tanks this was going to be a laugh

OH—

Stephanie over there lying completely still with Bett's dad leaning over her why wasn't he over here checking on Bett and there was an EMT and Mrs. Roan screaming at her father with no sound.

PART TWO

15

Autumn, Monday, Day Three of This Already God-Awful Year of Eleventh Grade

MONDAY MORNING, BETT WOKE IN HER ROOM, WHICH was freezing again, regardless of September and regardless of the endless walls of books. That's what the wind would do, she guessed. Her shower was blistering cold, too—her mom hadn't figured out how to get the water heater to work well enough to heat the water all the way yet, so first come, first to get the better, tepidish stream, while the second shower-taker always stood under the water purpled with goose pimples. But today Bett didn't care. She had bigger things to worry about, such as how was she going to avoid that Eddie and that bus? Because the more she thought about it, the more weirded-out she was. What kind of talk could pamphlet-flinging Eddie possibly want to have that wouldn't be mortifying, upsetting, or angrymaking in some way? Well, a big old *no* to that. The bus was to be avoided at all costs.

She didn't hear any movements in the teeny house, but if her mother hadn't left yet, there was no way Bett could skip the bus, because, from the small tower she had made as her own room, Bett's mom could see the bottom of the slope where Bett was supposed to wait. But if her mom was already gone and at the station house, Bett might have a chance to skip the bus and go through the woods instead, and then meet the road and make her way to school on foot. She'd be super late, but who cared? Anything was better than getting on that bus with Eddie. Even going to school through the woods with a picture-slashing fire-burner lying in wait at Salt River K–12.

It was so chilly, Bett had a good excuse not to wear shorts, but she wore them anyway. She knew that if she walked or, God help her, ran in the cold, her thighs would turn purple and blotchy like a plucked chicken ready for the oven, so she grabbed another old-man thrift-store sweater, brown this time, to wear on top, and called it a day because there was no way she was getting on that bus with that snarp of a bus driver who wanted to talk to her, because she knew what the topic must be—fathers or food—and there was no way she was going to discuss either.

"Well, well, well, my princess is woken by the pea and comes downstairs." Shoot. Her mother *was* still home, in uniform, and in fine form. *Damn. Come on.* "Good morning, toots."

"My room barely fits a twin bed with one mattress, never mind a stack," said Bett.

"Next time I'll build a mansion," said her mother, dumping yesterday's cold coffee from the pot down the sink. "Remind me to do that the next time I do touch-ups on the place."

"It's freezing in here," said Bett.

"If only there were some way to get wood into the woodstove and build a fire," said her mother, glancing at the woodpile in the corner. "Ah, well. Some dreams are meant to be unfulfilled. Speaking of fire, watch out at that school today. You text me right away if anything else happens. I'll be up at the school myself later, working the case."

Great.

Bett shrugged with nerves and impatience. "Whatever," she said. "I have to go."

"Not before you eat some oatmeal at least," said her mother.

"I'll bring a Pop-Tart," said Bett, and before her mother could argue about oatmeal, she was out the door and on her way down the slope, having expertly palmed three foil casings of Pop-Tarts out of the box and taken her three sodas out of the fridge. The nervejangle inside her was growing, and she knew the Pop-Tarts could quiet at least enough of it to get her to school on this stress-morning.

Now that her mother was still there up in the house, would Bett have to come up with some kind of backup plan for escaping the bus unnoticed? She thought for a minute.

No, she would just have to chance it.

So, backpack on, Bett shifted her way through the woods, following the route of the road but parallel to it. The familiar chug of diesel filled the air, and Bett panicked like a five-year-old and wondered how to hide. This section of the woods had had a fire some years ago, so all the trees in it were new ones like birches and aspens, not exactly wide enough for a Bett to hide behind. She settled for luck and crouching, and kept moving steadily down through the trees. Her brown sweater was smart, actually, kind of like camo, even though the birches were white and gold and silver. Never mind. She heard the bus wait and wait, and then give her up for absent and go on its way, passing her with its diesel stink and Ranger's concerned face looking blankly out the window.

It took Bett longer to reach the school than she'd thought it would, mainly because by the time the bus had passed and she could get on the road, there was no way to get there fast enough because if she ran, she knew from yesterday it would be too Plus and she'd spend all day having to undo it. The Pop-Tarts were a good way to undo today's walk if she ate all six on the way to school, which she did, hating herself with every bite even as she popped the last one in her mouth as she climbed the stairs to the entrance to Salt River K–12.

But being late to school didn't matter today. Everyone was crowded in the main hall and Bett went into instant panic mode. What the hell was going on? She saw Dan's loose-boned, easygoing self, in his gray hoodie with the skull on the back, standing in the crowd, and made her way over to stand a ways behind him. At least Dan didn't look terrified, so maybe it wasn't anything bad.

It was the opposite of bad. Anna was on a stepladder. Around her shoulder was a clear plastic bag of papers, covered in color and shadings, papers she had clearly dipped in paint and something more that made them stiff and curled at the ends. She was placing the paper slices carefully on the wall, building them up until she was almost done and everyone could see that the wall in the hallway was now filled with a giant pair of wings. They were gorgeous— green, blue, purple, red, yellow. Bett pressed forward with everyone else.

What was that? The edge of that wing looked familiar, colors bleeding into each other but curled and crisped brown at the ends. Then Bett got it. These were all the slashed, burned-up pictures from the first day of school, and Anna had transformed them into this glorious, feathered explosion of color flight.

Not with permission, though. The principal picked his

way through the crowd. "Anna Reed," he said, "what do you think you are doing?"

"Fixing things," said Anna, her thin caddis-house body all in black layers, with some bits of the curled drawing-feathers stuck in her hair.

"Who gave you permission to take student materials? Those destroyed pictures were evidence," said the principal. "In my office. Now."

The roar of protest surprised even Bett, who agreed with it but didn't expect everyone to care.

"That ass better not make her take them down," said Dan. He was firm but still so *calm*. It almost irritated Bett. Hadn't he been full of scaredish commentary about all this on the bus? But now Bett thought about him from when they were younger, even then so calm and peaceable in most situations. He had been the same way in ninth grade when their group had fought during some Social Studies project or other. And when she thought about it, even when Dan argued with Ranger it was small, calm waves that actually seemed to move their brotherhood forward.

To be honest, it all kind of pissed Bett off.

16

Autumn, Monday, Day Three of Eleventh Grade, Gym, of All Things

IT WAS AFTER HOMEROOM AND ANNA AND HER WINGS. Time for gym, and Bett was not going to have anything to do with that.

"I have my period," she lied to Mrs. Brewster when attendance was over. Mrs. Brewster raised her eyebrows, but short of making Bett prove it, what was she going to do?

"You should probably get that checked out," said Mrs. Brewster. "You had your period almost all the time last year, too."

"I'll talk to my mom," Bett promised mendaciously, and took a seat on the bleachers to watch the class. The day's activity was rope-climbing, and Bett couldn't stop herself from remembering the rough feel of the rope in her hands, feet twisted and pumping up and holding her so she could get the next hand grasp, flying up up up until she touched the ceiling with one hand, always the first kid up, always the fastest, always the fastest to touch the ground after flying back down, too. But nope, no more of that. Bett leaned away from her own competence like some people leaned away from working hard in gym because sweat would mess up their hair.

Strength. It made you look so competent, like you were fine and could be left alone. And you were not fine. You were not fine fine fine.

17

Monday, Third Day of Eleventh Grade,
Lunch

BETT WAS ALONE AT LUNCH TODAY. RANGER WAS A couple of tables over, waving his lunch cake about and talking animatedly with a group of his friends, most of them, she couldn't help but notice, on the smallish side like Ranger. Bett was glad he was with friends, even though she missed the little bug. His conversation was something. *Somethingcakes.*

"Where were you this morning?" Dan asked, startling her as he plopped beside her at her table.

Talk like a normal person. Talk like a normal person this minute.

"Missed the bus," Bett said finally, and stared at her pizza. Was Dan sitting with her because he felt sorry for her for being alone?

"Oh," said Dan. "Well, you were lucky. You missed rendition six million and twelve of the Eagles' 'Hotel California.' Do you know how long that song is?"

Bett did. It was, of course, a staple in her mother's playlist.

"Though it can't be any longer than 'Bohemian Rhapsody,'" said Dan, "which my dad blasts at all hours."

Was this a conversation? Was Bett trapped in an actual conversation? Did she have to say something or could she just get the message across that she didn't want to talk by being silent?

"Don't get me wrong, it's good song," said Dan. "But not after the six million and twelfth time you hear that one, too."

"I bet they're going to take Anna's art down," Bett said awkwardly. A non sequitur, but at least it was speech.

"Maybe," said Dan. "I think they'll give her detention at the minimum." He swallowed. "That picture-fire thing keeps making me think about loners and kids with guns in high schools and all that shit."

Bett couldn't respond out loud. But she nodded.

Dan took out his pocketknife and expertly trimmed the crusts of his pizza off the slices. "No more carbs than necessary."

Bett started before she could help herself.

"I was only doing an impression of my mom," said Dan. "I just hate the crust."

Bett picked up her own lunch cake and began to eat. *Please make him stop talking*, she thought as she bit off more and more cake.

"You're good with my brother," said Dan abruptly. "The little dude really likes you."

What? Bett coughed. "He's cute," she said finally. "I like him, too."

"Well, I think it's nice."

And now Bett couldn't think of another thing to say. All her words were spent.

She left the lunch table before Dan was done. She didn't want him to think he was stuck with her, and plus, she had to see if the wings were still there. And they were, their bright, burned colors transforming the dark, old hallway into something better than the smell of kids and books and teachers that had seeped into its bones. Anna and Hester and a couple of their Twinkler friends were there, too.

"Two days of detention," Anna was telling them.

"No way!"

"Come on!"

"Is he going to make you take it down?"

"He said he isn't sure," Anna answered.

"WTF?" said a Twinkler.

WTF is right. That's insane, thought Bett. *This is the loveliest thing we've ever had in this school. He should be, like, paying her.*

"Wait," said Hester. "Look. What's that?" She pointed above the flowering wings.

Above Anna's work was a new picture, done on regular 8½ x 11 school paper. It was very rough and in Sharpie and who knew what it was supposed to be, but it looked like a devil head breathing out a cone of fire, only with the flames drawn out smooth rather than jagged as one would normally depict them.

WARNING, it said under the devil head. WE'RE WATCHING YOU.

"Who would do that? Why?" It was Anna, being led away from her wings and to the main office by her friends. Bett knew her mother was in that office with McLean, talking about the vandalism. Bett hoped the case would be solved soon, and her mother tucked safely back at the station house, where she belonged.

"What's Anna's problem?" asked Dan, who had left the caf as well and was standing beside Bett. "And where'd you go? I thought we were talking."

Bett said nothing, but she gestured at the picture above the wings.

"What?" Dan looked up but remained mystified. "At least the principal didn't do a psycho himself and tear Anna's project down. She must have stayed up all night making those feathers."

Bett pointed again. "Not the wings," she managed at last. "That picture thing. Above them."

The devil breathing fire really was intensely creepy. It was clear Dan thought so, too, frozen in place and staring.

"Fairly psycho," said Dan at last. His eyes followed Anna across the foyer. "But I bet it's harmless."

"It's *not* harmless," said Bett. All those school shootings in the news, and here was some maniac destroying art and then putting up a devil image over the new piece that was made to replace it. "That's a signature."

"What's a signature?" asked Dan.

"Something a perp leaves at the scene of the crime to mark their work." Why was it easier to talk cop talk than to talk like a normal teenage girl? If she was channeling her mother, that shit better stop right now.

Then: *We can't let Ranger see*, but she knew there was no way of protecting him from it.

Dan look puzzled. "What do you mean? You think Anna signs her work with devils? Not exactly in character, no?"

"No. Not Anna. The *destroyer* left the signature."

"Oh," said Dan. He paused. Then: "That's effed up but . . . sort of interesting."

So the picture-slasher-burner had a signature. Huh.

Well, I know one perp who ought to have hired out the job, Bett thought. *That is a hell of a badly drawn devil.* She knew she was fronting, though. Things were only going to escalate from here.

18

Monday,
End of Day Three of Eleventh Grade

AT THE END OF THE DAY, BETT WAS DOWN THE STEPS and in front of the bus before she realized that her plan had been to walk home, just as she'd walked to school. And it would be even easier this afternoon, since her mother was back at the station house and wouldn't be there to grill her. But instead there was Eddie, hand on his door handle, staring down at her through those filmy eyes.

"No," said Bett.

Eddie was silent.

"I am not getting on this bus unless you leave me alone." Bett was startled to hear the words coming out of her own mouth, but glad enough about them to see what she would say next. "I am not talking about . . . anything."

Eddie stared at Bett.

Bett stared at Eddie.

"Where were you this morning?" Eddie asked. "During the morning ride? You have an appointment or something?"

But Bett knew that Eddie knew that she hadn't had an appointment.

"I got you over a barrel," said Eddie finally. "You don't get on this bus, I place one call to your mother to discuss where you were this morning and what you were doing and that's it. I know what a tough cookie one Officer Marianne Gaffney is."

Bett tried to snort but couldn't because the man was right, and there was no way Bett was discussing anything about anything with her mom. He did have her over a barrel.

"I'll get on the bus," she said at last. "As long as you don't talk about—stuff."

Eddie looked at her and exhaled sharply. His eyes looked filmier.

"Fine," he said. "Get the hell on my bus."

Bett got the hell on his bus.

Once the boys were on the bus and they were on their way, Bett let her head rest against the window. Was this how it was going to be, every day, on the bus? Afraid that Eddie was going to open his mouth? Because if he was, Bett was going to tell her mom to forget it. Pretend she wanted to walk to school. She was older now and could handle weirdos, and also Bett knew her mom might even be glad, even hope that Bett would not walk but jog to school and get back to being a badass. But would walking to school, no matter how slowly (which was how Bett would do it), be too Plus? And was that Plus worse than Eddie and his weight noticings or father advice hanging over her head every day?

First the school crazy and now the Eddie crazy. Too much crazy for one person to bear. Bett rummaged in her backpack and came up with two fun-size candy bars and ate them in quick succession.

"What's going on?" It was Dan, but he wasn't talking to her. Bett looked up.

What is *going on?* Because instead of looping to the left down along the river, sloshing brown and hectic, Eddie had banked right and was driving along the other road, the one leading away out of the woods here and into the land area that was still farms.

"Yo!" said Mutt. "You're going the wrong way, dude."

"No," said Eddie. "I'm not. We're *doing* this."

"Doing what?" asked Ranger, draping himself over the seat in front of his.

But Eddie didn't answer, and hunched over his wheel like he was driving a tank.

"Holy hell," said Dan, and leaned out into the aisle, eyes on the road unfolding in front of the bus. "This is it. He's flipped and he's going to kill us all!"

Oh my effing God. I just called him crazy in my mind,

but I didn't mean it literally. And now he literally is. My own mother a cop and I'm the one getting kidnapped. I missed all the signs.

What signs?

What wasn't *a sign, Bett?* Eddie was a walking bundle of signs. Crazy vet with crazy in his eyes. *Oh my God, we're all going to die.*

"Eddie!" Ranger's voice was high. "What are you doing? Are you kidnapping us?"

"Yep," said Eddie.

"What?" Ranger yelped.

"I said, 'Yep.'"

"Eddie, come on." Even Mutt sounded nervous. "What are you talking about? What the hell are you doing?"

"I told you. I'm kidnapping you."

"Eddie!" Dan glanced at Ranger, who was blinking. "Cut it out."

"I will not cut it out. Shut up." The bus was running along a wooden fence lining one of the fields.

"Where are you taking us?" Dan's voice was strained.

But Eddie was silent and he drove the bus straight ahead, unyielding and piston strong. Until finally, for the third time in three school days, he stopped short.

"Here," he said amidst the ensuing tumble of backpacks and food wrappers. "Everyone get out."

What was going on? Terrified. Terrified. Slowly, Bett reached her hand into her bag for her phone. If she kept it low, he wouldn't see in the mirror.

"BETT! I SAID OUT! GET IN THAT FIELD!"

Bett let go of her phone.

"Is he, like, going to execute us?" Ranger whispered. His eyes were round and his neck looked impossibly thin.

"Don't worry," said Dan, calming, calming. "Take your backpack." And the four of them grabbed their packs and got out.

"Why are we going along with this?" said Mutt, and even *his* voice wobbled a little as they walked into the middle of the field.

Bett shielded her eyes from the low sun and tried to make a plan in her head. Never let the kidnapper take you to a second location, Bett knew. But how was she supposed to have known that had been part of Eddie's plan? Was this some weird way of Eddie's to try to get her to listen to him? In front of all the other kids?

Bett's stomach roiled. *Think, Bett.* Could she get her phone out and call her mom without Eddie noticing now?

Nope. Not yet. The four of them watched as Eddie approached them, waving a duffel bag he brought from the bus.

"Is it guns in there? Is it guns?" Ranger's voice was terrified. Dan put his arm tight around his brother's shoulder.

"Of course not," Dan said, again calm, calm. Bett glanced at him. He shrugged back at her, eyes glancing meaningly down at the top of his little brother's head.

Eddie cleared his throat. "I guess you kids wonder why I've brought you here."

Bett was afraid to even nod.

"Are you going to kill us?" asked Ranger. His chin was quivering, and he burst into tears.

"Jesus Christ!" Eddie yelped. "What's with the waterworks? What the hell is the matter with you?"

"You're kidnapping us," sobbed Ranger, and Mutt stepped forward and stuck his chest out at Eddie.

"I can take you, old man," he said. "I got six inches and sixty pounds on you." He moved back and forth in front of Eddie and shoved his chest in Eddie's chest.

I hope there's no bomb in there, Bett thought desperately, and she ran up to the duffel bag and kicked it as hard as she could.

Everybody turned to watch the bag as it described a perfect, long arc and landed fifty yards from the terrified group.

"YES!" shouted Dan, and he muscled up to Eddie, too. "Bett is strong as shit, asshole," he said in Eddie's face. "She and I will *take* you."

"What is the matter with you kids? What the hell has gotten into you? You just can't kick my property like that!"

"Says the psycho, phone-throwing man who kidnapped us!" Dan yelled back.

Ranger gulped noisily, sobbily, in the background.

"I did not!" Eddie shouted back. "Okay," he said, "okay.

I threw a phone. But come on. That was a couple of days ago. And you aren't *kidnapped*."

"You said we *were*!" cried Ranger.

"Yeah," said Mutt. "Why else are we here?"

"Against our will!" Dan added.

"Jesus Christ," said Eddie. "Jesus Christ! I was kidding when I said about the kidnapping! A figure of speech, for God's sake. I'm not a stranger! You kids know me!"

"Most abductions happen with people known to the victim," said Bett, breathing heavily.

Dan and Ranger looked at her with . . . respect.

Bett shrugged. "My mom's a cop."

"Call her!" screamed Mutt.

"Oh my God," moaned Eddie. "Don't call her!"

"See! You *are* kidnapping us!" cried Ranger, his voice growing damp again. "You're controlling our phone use! You're an abductor! That's what they do!"

"I am not! Fine! Call her! All of you all call who you want." Eddie gestured grandly. "There. I just gave you permission to use your phones on school time and property."

"THIS IS NOT SCHOOL TIME OR PROPERTY!" shouted Mutt. "WE SHOULD BE HOME RIGHT NOW ON OUR TIME AND OUR PROPERTY, BUT YOU GODDAMN KIDNAPPED US!"

Eddie's shoulders sank. "Kids," he said. "Kids. If you'd have just let me explain before you started crying around and kicking my bag."

"I am on you like green on grass, old man," said Mutt, and he continued to yak-chest his way onto Eddie.

"No," Eddie said. "Please. Hear me out. It's kinda you who sparked this, Mutt." He blew air through pursed lips. "You run like a damn gazelle, kid."

Mutt pushed Eddie. "Perv!"

"No," said Eddie. "Not like that. For God's sake. I may have kidnapped you a little, but I'm no perv." He breathed heavily again. "It's like this. You know how we're a real small school."

What the hell? But they nodded.

"And it's hard to get coaches. AND teams. For sports."

"Mr. Grisley," countered Mutt. "Field hockey. Basket-ball."

"Yeah," said Eddie. "Grisley does those. What you might not know, see, is that I was a real athlete when I was your age. And older." He broke off and coughed.

"Was that before you started smoking, or after?" Dan asked.

"Shut the hell up. Before." Eddie wiped his mouth. "Anyway. My thing was running. And there was this notice from your principal the other week about how great it would be for the school to have cross-country. Only there was no coach. And could we spread the word. And I thought to myself, well, I could do that. But it would mean more time with twerpy kids—"

"Hey," said Ranger.

"—with twerpy kids," Eddie repeated firmly. "And the pay sucks."

"Does it suck more than bus pay, Eddie?" asked Ranger. His voice sounded almost back to normal.

"Sucks even worse," said Eddie. "It's, like, nominal. So I said to myself, Eddie, it's not worth it. But then . . . " He shook his head. "You kids. You four. None of you already doing football or field hockey. None of you too twerpy. Mutt, you running. You on that bus and you two boys." He nodded toward Dan and Ranger. "Thin and stringy, perfect for distance running. And then Bett came on the bus this year. You." He gestured at Bett but didn't meet her eye. "You're built—real strong."

Shut up about how I'm built!

"Not to mention you ran up that slope the other day like a mother— like a very good runner," Eddie amended.

Dan glanced at her. Bett stared at the ground.

"And it was like a sign," Eddie continued. "You all on the bus and Mutt running and Bett here booking it up that hill like a catamount. We need four to be a team, and with the Title Nine stuff I can let Bett count."

What was he talking about? A team? Then Bett's thoughts skittered to, *Oh, how great, I get to count.*

"So we aren't kidnapped?" said Dan.

"*No,*" said Eddie. "I'm explaining. Shut up a minute."

"*You* shut up a minute!" shouted Mutt. "You're the one scaring us to death with your crazy vet ways."

There was silence.

"Don't you ever," said Eddie, and his voice was deadly, "call me that again."

"Don't you ever kidnap me again!"

"I'M NOT KIDNAPPING YOU! I'm working with you! The four of you! I'm letting Bett on!"

"Letting Bett on what?" Dan asked.

"On our team. ON our TEAM, dammit! What do you think I'm talking about?" Eddie grinned nervously. The four of them stared unsmiling back at him. "Hold on," said Eddie, and he sprinted over to where his duffel had landed.

"He does have good speed," Mutt observed.

"Why are we still here?" Dan wondered. "What's the matter with us?"

"He's got the keys to the bus," said Bett.

"Good point," said Mutt. Bett ignored him.

"He kidnapped us to be on a team? A track team?" asked Ranger. He sounded less scared, thank God.

"I think so," said Bett.

"Cross-country, more like," said Dan. "What a way to do it." His eyes were still locked on Eddie.

But now Eddie was back. "Look," he wheezed.

"Quit smoking, Eddie," said Dan.

"Shut up." Eddie opened the duffel. "Four shirts. One for each of you. All men's extra large because I wanted to make sure they would work for everyone. You," he said, "are my new team. Welcome to the Salt River Cross-Country Fishermen."

"I'm no man," said Bett.

"Be a Fisher*person*, for God's sake, then!" Eddie shouted. "I don't care! Cross it out and write in what you want."

"I got a Sharpie in my backpack," offered Ranger.

Mutt waved away Eddie's and Ranger's words with a meaty hand. "I'm not joining your goddamn team," he said to Eddie.

"Come on," said Eddie. "Come on! You're born to it, Mutt. I can really make something out of you."

"I'm already making something out of myself," said Mutt.

"I'm not joining either," said Dan. "Why do we have to be the four? You can't just kidnap us to an open field and then think we're going to do you a favor by joining your cross-country team."

"Do me a favor? Do *me* a favor? Everything I ever learned in life I learned in sports. Teamwork. Discipline. This shit would do YOU a favor."

"I'm sure," said Dan. "I'm sure team sports really made a man of you, Eddie. Really made you into the person you are today. Great. But no. I hate running, I want to do tech for the fall play, and I'm not doing this."

"Come on, Dan! Who's been driving you to school on and off since you were a little twerp? Who came all the way back to the school to get you and take you home when you forgot to get on the bus that day in first grade?"

"You're the one who drove off without me, Eddie," said

Dan. "There I was, waving my arms like a maniac on the sidewalk, and you just drove—"

"Regardless, Dan. Regardless. I can make you love running. I can make you wake up and want to get your sneakers on your feet before your eyes are even open."

"Why do you even want to? Shit pay and we all are pretty twerpy," said Dan.

"I'm not twerpy," said Ranger, but Dan ignored him and continued: "What's in it for you?"

But before Eddie could answer, Ranger spoke up again. "I'm never being on a team with you, Eddie. You scared me to death. I, like, cried in front of people."

Dan moved and put his arm around Ranger again.

Ranger's voice trembled, but he forged on. "You don't want us to call you crazy, but you scared us so hard we almost died."

Eddie shifted uncomfortably. "You got a point," he said. "I apologize. Okay? I apologize. I really do. I just see real potential in you all. It means something to me." He cleared his throat. "It's kinda moving."

"Moving," said Mutt disgustedly.

"Well," said Ranger, seemingly in spite of himself, "I *would* look goodcakes in that shirt. Wicked goodcakes." And he wrestled the team shirt on over his clothes and looked down at himself with the start of something like pride blooming.

"Goodcakes," sneered Mutt.

"I do look goodcakes," said Ranger, and pulled the shirt away from his stomach to look at the mascot fish swimming cheerfully across it. He dropped it, and the hem skirted his knees. Bett snort-laughed. Then she froze. She hadn't laugh-snorted like that since . . . *No.*

Dan looked tactfully away, but he laugh-snorted, too. Bett's shoulders shivered for a second, but then she was okay. She was fine.

"I'm not doing it," Mutt was saying. "I work after school. I can't stay two and a half extra hours every day after school to practice and then work, too."

"What's this work you do?" asked Eddie.

"Lawns," said Mutt.

Eddie rolled his eyes. "Lawns," he said. "Kid, in two weeks nobody's mowing their lawns anymore until spring. You'll have all kinds of time."

"Then I have to find something else," said Mutt. "Eddie, I have to work, because come basketball, which is my real sport, I can't work again anyway, and I have to earn what I can now."

Eddie squinted. "I got it," he said at last. "You can be my assistant."

"Why does he get to be the assistant?" cried Ranger. "Does he get a *uniform*?"

"He gets a little prestige. And a little cash. They said I could have an assistant," said Eddie. "For nominal pay," he hastened to add. "But it's something."

"I'll do it!" said Ranger. "Let me do it, Eddie! Why does it have to be him?"

"Because," said Eddie, "I told you. The kid *runs*. Like a goddamned *gazelle*. You can all learn from him."

"It pays?" said Mutt. "Because I got a clientele."

"For two weeks more, tops, you got a clientele," said Eddie. "Then nada. Finish them on Sundays. Our first meet isn't until Saturday."

"What!"

"That's not even a week!"

"They come up quick," said Eddie. "Most teams start practice in the summer. Don't worry about this one. We'll take it as a practice meet. And Mutt, you'll get overtime pay for it."

Mutt looks at him steadily. Then, "Well," he said. "Okay. Running's better than most other work I could find, probably."

"It *will* be better," said Eddie.

"Fine," said Dan. "Whatever. Me too. I can do the winter play. I'm supposed to watch out for Ranger after school anyway."

"You are not, you smerchface! Shut up!"

"Yes, I am, turd."

"I'm in seventh grade!" fumed Ranger, his face growing red.

But Eddie didn't care. "Yes!" he said, and punched the air a little. "And how about you?"

Everyone turned to Bett. She felt huge in her grandfatherly sweater and shorts.

Bett shrugged. She opened her mouth, but she only managed a grunt. How could she do this when it was nothing but pure Plus? And yet, she loved . . . *No.*

"Is that a yes?" Dan asked.

Bett cleared her throat. "I have to call my mom," she said. "She's probably like *what the hell* since I haven't gotten home, anyway."

"Sure," Eddie said grandly. "All you kids. Call your folks. Tell 'em I got you."

19

Monday Afternoon, Still Weirdly in the Field

"YOU'RE JOINING THAT TEAM," BETT'S MOM DECLARED when Bett finally reached her, still at the station house. "Especially after all this I hear about you getting to school late because you missed the bus? And walked to school on your own?"

"*Mom*," said Bett. This rotten town was so damn small. Eddie, Mrs. Schlovsky in the office, her mother at the school to work on the psycho case. One conversation with her mom would be all it took.

But then Bett was quiet.

So was her mother. Then: "Do it, baby. Why don't you just do it?"

Bett was silent again. Her mother's voice firmed up again. "You're doing it. At least then I'll know you are where you say you are, when you are."

Her mom did have her over a barrel. First Eddie. Now her. Whatever. Bett could always refuse to run and just walk, couldn't she? She was only a body they needed to count.

"Fine," said Bett, and hung up.

"She's making me," she said to Eddie, and then, accepting a Sharpie from Ranger, Bett leaned down over the grass and crossed out the "-men" in "Fishermen" on her T-shirt and wrote in "people" above it instead.

Dan took the Sharpie from her and did the same.

Bett looked at him, shocked. Then she reddened and turned away.

20

Autumn, Tuesday Morning,
Day Four of Eleventh Grade

I was kidnapped, and now I am on a sports team. It was a hell of a first thought to have in the morning when she woke up. But have it Bett did, and the weirdness of the previous day stuck with her through the morning bus ride. On the one hand, the team was about running, which was too Plus. But on the other, equally awful hand, it was more exposure to Eddie and his wanting to talk to her. He had a better chance of that if he had time with her every day after school. And Bett was scared enough already of the impending Plus running, because if that was wrapped up in some Eddie plan about her weight, too, what was she going to do?

Her mother was acting like this was the best thing to happen to their family since they'd moved into the SIM card house.

"You'll get back to yourself," she had told Bett at dinner last night. "Girl, you got talent, and you've been wasting it. Do what God put you on this earth to do."

Bett sighed, but inside she was terrified. If she did what she was good at, so many Pluses would build up that the aftermath would be hell.

After the morning bus ride, Ranger and his little group of friends ran into the school building, all of them talking together in fierce whispers. As they moved inside and muttered in their intense way to one another, one of them held his left hand high in the air, only to have it slapped down by Ranger, who looked around as if to see if anyone noticed. Bett had no idea what he was up to, but it was something. Cakes.

Paul was at Bett's table in English class, along with Hester and Hester's best friend, Lily, and a couple of others. Doug, one of Mutt's meat-minions, was at the table behind them. "Let me explain the first part of our semester today. We'll start with our first author study," Ms. Peters, the teacher, said. They had had Ms. Peters last year in tenth grade, too. "Virginia Woolf. She's one of my favorites."

It all sounded very dull. Bett zoned out until Ms. Peters ended her drone about Virginia Woolf's life and books and overbearing father and having rooms of one's own. "She was very depressive," Ms. Peters told them, going around the tables, passing out books. "In the end, it was too much for her, and she filled her pockets with stones and walked into the water and drowned."

"Damn," said Paul. He was tall and thin and dressed in a wild way, in a lavender checked suit and bow tie. Bett supposed he was glad he was at their table and not with the homophobic Doug. But Doug was sitting too close for comfort anyway. "What a way to do it."

"God," said someone else from the back of the room. "Why would you?"

Hester shuddered. "It must have taken forever. She must have breathed in water for, like, ten minutes before she died."

But Ms. Peters was going on now about language and alliteration. Bett looked at her knees and wiggled her hematite toes a little in her sneakers.

"Everybody read the first few pages of the book," Ms. Peters said. "See what you think about the language. Can you find any alliterative moments?"

This was why English class bit. Teachers sucked the life out of a story before you could even get into it with all the analyzing. Why couldn't the kids just read something and then talk about what they thought of it?

"We have a psycho in our school, and all she wants to talk about is alliteration?" Doug said to the kids at the table behind her.

"Shut up, Doug," said Lily, turning around. "I'm, like, trying not to think about all that."

"Don't worry, Lily," Doug continued, throwing a

crumpled-up piece of paper at her. "We got you. We'll smash the person behind this."

"Not if they kill us first," said Hester. "Jesus."

Ms. Peters went on rustling papers at her desk as if she'd heard nothing. Bett hated her.

"Did you hear?" Dan caught up with her at her lunch table again.

"I'm not deaf," said Bett.

Dan started. "What are you talking about? And besides, aren't you?"

"What the hell?" said Bett as they plopped down at the table. "My hearing is fine. Mostly. Sometimes my left ear goes out. But yes, I heard what Doug and Lily were talking about in English class, and it's nothing we aren't all thinking anyway."

"I don't know what you're talking about," said Dan. "Why are you such a grump?"

Bett stared at her lunch, stomach churning from all her talking. Then: "Doug and Lily? Talking about the psycho? Why do we all keep coming back here if someone's about to go off at any minute?"

Dan looked at her. "I know," he said. "You're right. But what I meant was, did you hear about the boys' locker room?"

"No," said Bett. "What are you talking about?"

"What I'm talking about is that there was another one

of those devil-breathing-fire pictures. Hung up over the lockers. We all saw it in gym second period."

"*What?*" Bett asked. "You're freaking me out even more!"

"We're all freaked out," said Dan, who was apparently not freaked out enough to stop chomping down his grilled cheese.

"Who the hell is doing this? Who *would?*"

"Someone who wants attention?" said Dan.

Bett shook her head. "No," she said. "Because it's anonymous. It must just be someone who wants to, like, have an effect on people. In a shitty way."

"Like that ass who called in the bomb threat last year."

"Yeah," said Bett. "My mom investigated that one and she said that was the psychology. Didn't help, though. She never caught whoever did it." Whatever the reason for all her speaking now, Bett was grateful that even if it wasn't Normal Girl talk, she was at least able to talk cop talk to Dan.

"I don't know if I'd want to catch who's doing these stupid pictures," said Dan. "The asshole would probably pin me to the ground and draw that devil on my face."

"Don't even," said Bett, glad that the main part of her lunch was eaten so she could start in on her cookies.

"A slasher-burner devil-drawer," said Dan. "What a weird combo."

*   *   *

Bett let Dan get ahead of her on the way out of the lunch-room. But both of them stopped when they saw Anna making repairs to some of the paper feathers she had made. At least the principal hadn't made her take the wings down in the end. Anna's work really was lovely. *Why can't I be more like her?* Bett thought. Why couldn't she be normal like Anna and speak reliably whenever she wanted to, and not just like some kind of cop in training? And Bett had to admit, as Twinkler as Anna was, she had balls.

Tuesday, Fourth Day of Eleventh Grade, Cross-Country Practice, Apparently

AFTER SCHOOL, EDDIE TOOK THE SAME TURN AS HE had the day before and led them into the same open field.

"Are we, like, trespassing?" asked Dan. "Whose field is this?"

Eddie waved Dan's worry away. "I know a guy," he said cryptically. "All right. We start with stretches. Cross-legged toe touches! Now!"

Everybody obligingly crossed their legs and bent over, except Bett, who had no intention of shoving her rear end in the air for a viewing.

"What the hell is wrong with you?" Eddie asked her.

Bett said nothing. She took a pen out of her bag, and sat down on the ground, heel on her opposite knee, and wrote NO on the sole of her sneaker. She darkened it with several passes of the pen while Eddie jabbered at her.

"Put that pen away and get up. You have to stretch," he said plaintively. "You're gonna get injured if you don't, and then we won't have enough kids on the team to run in the meets."

"No," said Bett levelly.

He stared at her. She stared back.

"Can we get up?" asked Ranger, his voice strangled from the downward dangling of his head.

"Yes," said Eddie, tearing his gaze away from Bett. "We're moving on to quads."

That one Bett had no problem with. Eddie looked at her, puzzled, but said nothing.

When the stretching was over, Eddie poked Mutt. "You're up, kid. Outline the course for us."

Mutt stood up with a clipboard. "Okay," he said. "We're going to do two laps of this field as warm-up. Then we're going out the field, right on the road, left on Cutter's Way, left again on Ridge Road, and two more lefts back to here. Got it?"

"How long is that?" asked Ranger.

"A ways," said Mutt vaguely.

"So we're, like, running in a circle?" said Dan.

"God, you're smart," said Mutt.

"Asshole," muttered Dan, but only Bett heard him. She wasn't going to run, anyway. Not for Eddie and certainly not for Mutt. She'd do a couple of the stretches, but then she was going to walk the course. She might be being forced to be on this team, but there was no way she was going to Plus herself into so many Ho Hos she'd get sick from the unPlusing of the run. She was already going to have to unPlus the walk.

"Okay, everybody, get going." Mutt blew a whistle.

"Who gave that douche a whistle?" muttered Dan as he jogged off, Ranger trailing a little behind him.

Bett walked.

"What the hell is your problem? Why are you being such a pain in my ass?" Eddie yelled at her.

"I don't think you're allowed to swear at us, Eddie," Ranger called back, but then even he was too far ahead of Bett and Eddie for it to make a difference.

Second walk around the field and then Bett turned right, as she'd been directed, still walking, moseying really, thinking her own thoughts. The ground was cold and rutted with mud that had hardened. Bett tried not to think about how much she would have enjoyed running on it, pacing the ground underneath her feet until she kicked the crap out of those boys.

Stop, she told herself. *Don't think your way into a thought Plus.*

Suddenly, behind her, a god-awful horn sounded, louder than a goose on steroids, accompanied by a familiar diesel chugging.

Eddie was chasing her with the bus.

N. GRIFFIN

"Move it!" he bellowed out the window. "You join a team to run, dammit, you *run!*"

"No," said Bett, and slowed her pace even further. But the bus picked up speed behind her and that awful honking began again. A car passed going the other way, and Bett had to move in front of the bus to let it go, her face burning because now she had to run, run at least faster than the bus creeping behind her before Eddie mowed her down, which he was so crazy he might just do, and there was the car full of people looking at her running and her butt cheeks were moving independently of each other, and the horror of it all made her want to run away from it, anyway, which only confused things because would that be a Plus or an act of self-preservation?

"GO!" screamed Eddie, leaning out his window. "And you better keep it up because I don't trust the brakes on this thing!"

Jesus! Bett picked up speed. Her legs stretched out and oh God, it felt good, but also terrifying because what if Eddie hit her, and then she thought maybe that would be okay because it would undo the Plus this run was turning into. How long had it been since she'd run? Really run?

But she knew exactly how long it had been.

Bett sprinted with the honking Eddie in pursuit until she caught up with Dan, who looked fearfully behind him as Eddie pressed on with his bus and his horn the rest of the way around the course until they reached the field again.

JUST WRECK IT ALL

"What was that?!" shouted Dan. "Are you going to do that to us every day?"

"Only to pains in my ass who won't run."

"You could have killed us!"

"Yup," said Eddie. "So Bett better pick it up next time. No telling how well I can control that bus at such a slow speed."

"I was running as fast as I could!" panted Dan.

"Bett wasn't," said Mutt.

"How do *you* know?" said Bett. She knew she sounded rude, but this time she was glad of it. Flipping Mutt. Except if she were honest with herself, the run had not been hard, racing over that rutted mud, her muscles working, stiff, then long and loose, just as she had remembered running being like from before, with the added frisson of Eddie terror pushing her faster, faster, faster.

Oh God, don't think about it. Don't Plus it. Too late, though. She already knew she would have to do a midnight raid on one of her hiding places and eat as many snack cakes as it would take to unPlus that run, numb her out, and force her still again, stomach swollen, lying flat again on her bed in the SIM card house. Until the numbness was replaced with self-hatred for what she had done, what she had become.

"All right," said Eddie. "Now we're going to stretch to cool down. Granted your permission, of course," he said to Bett.

Bett said nothing.

"We're going to do, ah, a cobra pose," said Eddie.

"What the hell is that?" asked Mutt.

"It's where you do like this." And Eddie lowered himself stiffly down onto the ground to lie flat on his stomach, and then reared back up from the waist so they all could look into his slightly embarrassed eyeballs.

"Where'd you learn thatcakes?" asked Ranger.

"It's, ah, yoga," said Eddie.

"Yoga?!" Dan scoffed. "Eddie, are you turning into one of the city people?" Bett looked at him with appreciation. Her thoughts exactly.

"Shut up," said Eddie, lumbering back to his feet, "and do it."

Bett could handle this one. She got down on the sweet-smelling grass of the field with the others.

"Lie flat," said Eddie, "until I tell you to rise."

Bett lay flat. It was very restful. She smelled dirt and grass and felt tiny bugs crawl up her wrists.

"Who do you guys think the burner-slasher is? Cakes?" Ranger's voice was muffled by the ground.

"When did I say to talk?" demanded Eddie. "Rise!"

Obligingly, the four of them reared back as Eddie had. *Uh-oh*, thought Bett. *This feels amazing. Cakes.*

"Can't he talk during this part?" asked Bett. She didn't like seeing the scared look on Ranger's face.

"Yeah," said Dan. "We're done with the hard part. Can't we, like, socialize now, at least?"

"Who cares who did it, anyway?" said Mutt. "So someone slashed a bunch of bad art and lit it up. Big deal. Why does it matter?"

"Because it does," said Dan.

"Why does it? Why does anything?" said Mutt. "I mean, you said yourself we just ran around in a three-mile circle. What for? We're right back where we started."

"That's because that's how you told us to run, dillhole," said Dan. "And it's also where the bus came back to. How else are we going to get home?"

"And your picture got slashed, too, Mutt. That was of your great-grandpa. In his military uniform. Don't you even care?" Ranger's voice was curious.

Mutt sighed. "Who cares. You make something good, gets wrecked every time. Look at Coyote Acres."

"Who made those?" asked Ranger.

"What, coyotes?"

"No, the house pits."

Mutt sighed. "Developers, idiot. And art isn't for straight boys, anyway."

"What the hell kind of bullshit is that?" Eddie barked. "I'm *ashamed* of you, Mutt. See me after practice!" Eddie glared at Mutt, then glanced at the rest of them. "Back down to the ground," he said, and they all obligingly relaxed back into the grass. "The bus would stay put if some people moved their asses with the gift God gave 'em."

Mutt snorted. "God," he said.

"Now steeple your rear ends in the air like a triangle,"

commanded Eddie. "That one's called downward-facing dog."

"How do you know all this yogacakes?" asked Ranger, sticking his skinny rear in the air.

"Never mind how I know," said Eddie. "Just do it."

Oh well, Bett might as well do it, too. No one could see her butt if they were all doing it. "You do it too," she said to Eddie. Eddie shrugged and assumed the position.

"You know, it's the devil pictures that make it all extra creepy," said Dan, steepling as commanded as well. "It makes it seem, like, satanic or something."

"Maybe they aren't devils," said Ranger uncertainly.

"Of course they are, dork," said Dan. "What else has horns and breathes fire? Even if the drawing looks like a kindergartner drew it?"

"Maybe that's why the slasher slashed the art, Ranger," said Bett. "Because they suck at it and are jealous of kids who can draw."

But Ranger's brow only furrowed.

"It can't be a kindergartner," said Ranger. "It has to be someone tall enough to reach that high of the wall." Then he reddened. "I mean, if you care about thinking about it. Which I don't. Cakes," he said hurriedly.

Oh, Jesus.

Ranger and his short posse chatting when they got off the bus. And then again, fiercely and secretively, at lunch. And now this prevarication.

Ranger was on the case.

It was exactly the kind of thing the kid would do. No way. Bett had to dissuade him. The person who'd wrecked the pictures was more messed up than an undersize seventh grader should be dealing with.

"I wouldn't worry about it," she reassured Ranger, her voice sounding weird with her cheeks sliding into her eyeballs from all this being upside down. Still, the position felt good after the arched back of the cobra pose.

Would you quit thinking things feel good?

"Reallycakes?" said Ranger. "You don't think someone is going to hurt us?"

"Of course not," said Dan.

"All right, you bastards. Get up. And get on the bus. Except you, Mutt. We need to have a talk."

They stood, and Dan cast a grateful look at Bett. She smiled smally back at him.

"Thanks," he said.

Bett nodded. Besides, now they had the gift of the vision of Eddie doing the cobra pose with them for the rest of their lives.

See what a shit she was? Mere days after Mutt's first public disgust of her on the bus, here she was, making fun of Eddie in her head. She was just as bad as Mutt.

22

Autumn, Tuesday,
Home After That Hell Practice at Last

BETT STOOD AT THE TOP OF THE SLOPE, NOT READY TO go in the house yet and face her mother, who'd be beaming around because Bett had exercised. But look: Bett was safe because there was her mother, far down along the road Bett had just left, rollerblading like a mad thing. Her mother had a helmet on, but her still-feathered eighties hair peeked out from below the helmet, the pyramid structure of its top hidden beneath the helmet, at least. No matter how often Bett begged her mother to let her do over her makeup or go with her to get her hair cut, her mother refused to update her look. "Worked for me then, works for me now," she always said. And even though Bett begged to differ—not even a cat eye? Just that awful blue eyeliner all the way around her mother's eyes, shrinking them into her head?—her mother had support from Aunt Jeanette, who was just a slightly smaller version of Bett's mom. Both of them were eighties girls, and not in a cool, retro way, either. Pathetic and even more awful in their boldness.

"Besides"—Aunt Jeanette always took up for her sister—"you never wear makeup anymore yourself, Bett. And you looked damn good in it, too."

"Not really," Bett mumbled, and always managed to get away before a conversation could start about her and makeup and looking good.

Anyway, with her mother clearly gone for a while, rollerblading like a superhero from thirty years ago, Bett turned the other way on the ridge and looked down at the river. The clouds were thickening and the wind was turning the leaves up and over so their silver undersides were exposed.

Bett stood and looked down at the river's edge for a while, knowing it was filled with stones and caddis houses. Then she bent over (*cross-legged toe touches!*) and picked up a tube-shaped stone that, even though it was way up here, looked like a little patchwork caddis house itself, but Bett wasn't sure it really was one. She slipped it into her pocket anyway and as she did, she knew she was being looked at by someone, someone to the left. It was an odd feeling to know that she was being watched. She turned and there, long down the river, was the man in waders from the other day. She wondered if he had seen her bend over to take the caddis house, but then she figured he was far enough away not to see her rear. Or to care, even. This thought was heartening, and Bett waved at him, hearing her mother's voice railing in her head about stranger danger and safety. The man waved back.

Oh!

Now Bett got it. She knew who the man was. He wasn't that saw-lending neighbor. Like Eddie, he also worked in the Vet Services Center with her dad. She didn't remember his name, but she remembered *him*. He was some kind of therapist for the vets and had always been very nice to her when she was little, smiling at her with those dark, kind eyes. Always looking at her like he was really listening, like he really cared.

She wished she could remember the man's name. She knew she'd known it once.

Bett shook herself. Her father and people to do with his life were the last things she wanted to think about right now.

But still. Bett held on to the caddis house in her pocket, staring after the man.

Then she started back to the house. She already had her plans to undo the Pluses of the day that night. It was the one good thing about the SIM card house. There were plenty of places to hide emergency food, mostly behind the stacks of books that lined the walls. Bett could hide individual snack cakes there and then pull all the books in the row forward and even them up so nobody would ever know there were Ho Hos lurking behind the books. Or, if her mother was around and Bett couldn't access her inside stash, she could climb out her bedroom window easy as pie, walk to one of her outdoor reserves, binge, come back, and climb back in, making no noise, without her mother even knowing. Easier here than in their old house, the one they sold, the one they lived in when her father was still around, which he was decidedly not anymore, the weakass.

Damn. Her left ear was out again. Why? Bett didn't know. But not even the river sound was loud enough to permeate the numbness there.

23

TWO YEARS AGO . . . *Stephanie is dead.*

Bett sat up. All around her was white and chaos and she could hear not one bit of it, not the motion and not her mother talking and bending over her to put her arms around Bett with Bett shoving those arms away, frantic, because Stephanie was dead.

"She's dead!" Bett screamed. "She's dead! I killed her!"

Bett screamed and screamed even though she couldn't hear herself or her mother trying to shout at her.

What had she done what had she done what had she done? *Oh God, help me! Please! Please, help me!*

The hospital was too white and too bright and terrifying. All that motion and action and Bett heard not one bit of it, not one.

Her mother grabbed a little pad of Post-its from the nurses' station and wrote as fast as she could and held Bett as tight as she could to help her stop screaming. Eventually, the screaming stopped and settled into sobbing, which went on and on and on, until Bett could finally read the Post-its.

Stephanie wasn't dead. She had lost her right eye, but she wasn't dead. She was in another part of the hospital, and Bett couldn't stop picturing what Stephanie must look like and oh my God OH MY GOD I DID THAT and the screams started again, even though Bett hardly knew it because she couldn't hear them.

Bett had some burns and she couldn't hear, but she was okay. After a few days she could stand up like normal and Bett was okay.

Where was her dad? He had been in her room when she first woke up, she knew, because she had seen him over her mother's shoulder in those screaming moments, his lips moving, too. But where was he now? They wouldn't let Bett go home yet and she couldn't hear and where was her dad?

Gone. He didn't tell her. Bett's mother had to do it. She still had the little stack of Post-its and she wrote Bett a terrible note about how her father was gone. He had left them. He had left Bett and her mother for Stephanie and hers. The disgusting, weak goat of a man didn't even have the guts to tell her himself. He made her mother do it. Bett was going home and Stephanie was staying in the hospital and Bett couldn't hear and her dad, in the middle of all this, decided it was the right time to leave them. Bett was never going to talk to him again.

If she thought about it, though, if she thought about it, even her father's leaving was as much Bett's fault as Stephanie's losing her eye was. Because if Bett hadn't done so many Fizzicle Feets that Stephanie wanted to try and if Bett hadn't jumped on that hose and there hadn't been that explosion, Bett's father wouldn't have come over there and seen Stephanie's beautiful, tiny mother, delicate even without wings, and fallen in love with her on the spot. It wouldn't have happened. But no. Bett had to go and explode, destroy all the world.

Bett dashed out of the too-sterile room and down the hall, hospital gown flapping, nurses and her mother calling after her, running after her, but Bett couldn't stop, wouldn't stop. It was glorious, this running, this making a break for it. It felt like everything. It felt like the world.

Bett stopped on a dime.

Felt glorious? Like the world?

Since when did she deserve to feel like that?

No. No more. Too good.

Too *Plus*.

She would never move again. Not a Fizzicle Feet, not a step, not an inch.

Her mother caught up with her and stood beside her as a nurse came at them with a wheelchair. Bett's brain was in a roil, terror and hell washing over her whole body until it felt like she was made of nothing but those feelings and that roil.

"Mom," Bett whispered. "Can I order some stuff to eat?"

24

Tuesday, Eleventh Grade, After School

HER FATHER WAS ALWAYS TRYING TO CONTACT HER, even now, two years after the explosion, but the hell with that. What kind of ass of a dad picked checking on someone else's daughter over his own after something like that?

He called probably every other day even now, texted her all the time, but Bett's mom was right. He was like a thirteen-year-old, and even Bett knew she didn't mean a thirteen-year-old like Bett had been. She meant a snappy, selfish thirteen-year-old who got crushes on tiny red-haired women with gorgeous eyes and delicate hands, and who didn't care who he hurt and didn't even come back for his clothes. Bett's mom had put them in garbage bags on the side of the road, and the next morning they were gone, but who knew who had gotten them, her dad or the garbage truck or some other person. Who cared? All that mattered was that Bett's stupid Fizzicle Feets had made her a people destroyer.

The hospital therapist Bett only agreed to talk to one time and her mother herself, incessantly, always saying things like:

"It could have happened at any time, Bett! That gas pump system was so old, a bird's breath could have made it blow!"

Her mother and Aunt Jeanette for months on end after Bett got home from the hospital. But Bett said nothing. That had been the good part of the deafness. She could pretend. And who cared? Their pastor always said the same thing, too, but nothing mattered when the truth was the truth. Bett had felt that hose under her feet.

"Talk to Stephanie," her mother begged, but the very thought made Bett want to run, until she caught the Plus in the wish and stopped herself. Completely. She could never face Stephanie again. There was no apology big enough in the world. Nothing that could make that empty right eye socket whole and seeing again. Nothing that would absolve Bett from the life she had ruined.

And seeing Stephanie would mean seeing her skinny goat of a father, and Bett was never going to do that again, either.

Now Bett palmed the caddis house in her pocket and gazed at the river, half hoping to see the man. She thought of Pluses and Ho Hos and this one girl in school who everybody knew cut herself, all the time, with scars running up her arms to the elbow.

The river was so calm and smooth in its motion today that Bett wanted to punch it, punch it so hard that waves would ripple and race to the shore, but she couldn't. Wouldn't let herself. She could only stand here with a stone in her hand, the hand in her pocket, and know that she still had a lifetime to pay for that jump on the hose.

25

Tuesday Evening After the Fourth Day of Eleventh Grade

THIS HOUSE WAS SO DAMN SMALL. BETT WAS UP IN HER tiny room, but she could hear every word of the conversation between her mother and Aunt Jeanette, who was here for dinner, which was going to happen in a minute, but this was the gossip hour, when her mother and Aunt Jeanette talked about everyone and everything, in the same way with the same gestures, and Bett usually enjoyed it but not today. She held the stone in her hand and wished for quiet.

"I saw the Floozy today," said Aunt Jeanette. Aunt Jeanette saw her sometimes because she worked near the insurance agency.

Bett's mother sucked her teeth.

"She looked bloated," said Aunt Jeanette.

"Cut the shit, Jeanette," said Bett's mother. "I don't

care. BETT!" she roared unnecessarily. "COME DOWN
AND EAT!"

Eat.

Bett had come in the house, anxiety and terror sloshing all
over her from the running, and started in her first hiding
place with the Ho Hos, and then she'd moved to the second hiding place behind the stereo in the living room and
eaten the cookies, but even that hadn't been enough to take
away the Pluses and to X out all the hell that was storming
in her mind so she'd gone to her third hiding place and
eaten the potato chips and then some corn chips from the
actual pantry with cheese on them, three rounds done
in the microwave, and finally that was enough and now
she was in her room, stuffed and lying on her bed, finally
thinking of nothing.

But she went down anyway.

"How was your day, kid?" asked Aunt Jeanette. Dinner was lasagna. Bett was repulsed by the smell of melty
cheese, but she worked through her square in spite of
that.

"It was a day," she said to Aunt Jeanette. "How was
yours?"

"You would not believe," said Aunt Jeanette, who ran
the office of a construction company. "This jagweed came
in today and wanted to change an order that was already
paid for and out on the truck. I told him *are you kidding*

me? and he said *does it look like I am? You people should have told me I was getting the wrong wood,* and I was like, *yeah, because we're all psychic here and know what your plans are without you even telling us.* And then he was like, *I'm gonna call your boss* and I said *you're looking at her* and he swore and stormed out. Tripped on the doorjamb, too, which I enjoyed."

"Jagweed down!" said Bett's mom, and despite her nauseated, too-full stomach, Bett laughed. Aunt Jeanette could tell a story, that was for sure.

"How was cross-country, Bett?" her mother asked.

Bett looked at her plate.

"What?" said her mom, looking at her with concern. "Did something happen after school?"

Bett shook her head. "No," she answered. "No psycho stuff. Just running." Then, quickly, to distract her mother before she could start going on about how great it was that Bett had exercised, Bett looked up and blurted: "But what *is* going on with that dillhole who destroyed all the art, Mom? Do you guys have any, like, leads?"

"You know I can't talk about an active investigation," said her mother. "Just know that we're working on it."

"It sucks," said Bett.

"It does," said Aunt Jeannette.

"It more than sucks," said her mother.

"Do you *have* to come talk to people up at school?" said Bett plaintively. "Can't you interview them at the station?"

"Not without cause," said Bett's mother. "What, am I harshing your cool, being up at your school?"

Harshing my cool. Bett couldn't bear the outdated slang. But outdated or not, it was the truth. Bett's cool was definitely being harshed. She needed to keep her mouth shut about the psycho devil pictures even though she knew her mom would be investigating that, too, and spending even more time up at Salt River K–12.

"No," said Bett. "It's just that I'm sure it's all nothing. Just someone borderline crazycakes."

Ranger was catching.

"Borderline?!" Aunt Jeanette sang-screamed, and she and Bett's mom were off, singing Madonna, while Bett groaned and tipped her head back until her throat poked up into the air in agony. But any amount of Madonna was worth it if her mother was distracted from thoughts of the vandalism case.

"I brought you something, Bett," said Aunt Jeanette, stopping her terrible singing at last. "It's a flat iron. My hair's too curly for it to work, but I thought it would be perfect for yours because you have that soft wave. You could try it on your bangs."

"No, thanks," said Bett automatically.

"Well, I'll just leave it here in case you change your mind," said Aunt Jeanette. "No point in it going to waste at my house when maybe you can use it."

26

Autumn, Tuesday Night, Late Late Late

BETT PRESSED PLAY.

"This one is going to be a sprite," said the girl's voice. "I want to make her delicate and winged. But not corny. I want it to be like her flying really matters."

The girl's hands took up the scissors and started to cut into some tulle. It wisped and wafted as she worked it with each cut.

"Ugh," said the girl. "The hell with that. I'll layer it over metal instead."

27

Autumn, Wednesday, the Fifth Day
of Eleventh Grade, in the Morning

THE NEXT MORNING, BETT GOT UP AND SHOWERED and stared at the flat iron Aunt Jeanette had brought. She held it in her hand and thought of the caddis house and the river at the bottom of the slope and then the leaves that had turned silver-side up.

Why not, she thought. So she dried her bangs and flat ironed them, and then trimmed their raggedy edges with the sharp bathroom scissors. Then she scooped the rest of her hair up in its customary messy topknot and went down the slope to the bus.

Bett was surprised to see Dan with a rolled-up poster tube on the bus. It didn't seem like him to bring in a picture from home. Ranger, maybe, but not Dan. Maybe it was a map or a poster for one of the classrooms or something.

Anything, for example, had to be better than "The Rocks in Our Rivers Make Our Waters Sing" type of posters weak-ass Ms. Peters had had up in that English room for a million years.

When they got off the bus, Eddie yelling at them to throw away their shit the next time he dropped them off because he liked a clean bus, dammit, and Bett was leaving wrappers all over the place, Bett saw that Dan was not the only one carrying something. There were ten or twelve other kids with things in their hands, all clustered around Anna at the entrance of the school. Anna was there in an outfit she had clearly made herself, patched pieces of what Bett recognized as Anna's old clothes, sewn together and hanging drapily in triangles over her bones. Dan and Mutt eyed each other again, in that yak-chesty way that boys did sometimes, and then each of them turned his attention to Anna, who clearly was the ringleader here.

What was going on? Bett hung back at the outskirts of the group.

"We're not letting the ass beat us," Anna was saying firmly. "Here's tape and Super Tack, you all." There were at least fifteen kids around her now, all with something in their hands. Bett and Mutt were the only ones standing on the fringe. "GO!"

And they went. Opposite Anna's wings, on the glass case that held the school's athletic trophies, Hester put up a picture done in pastel of her mother, her mother caught in a moment of looking tired and spent after a day of work.

Why do all the bitchy ones get to have a talent? Bett wondered.

Other kids attached shadow boxes to the wall with Super Tack, boxes full of tiny, cherished items like rune stones and wee china teacups. When they ran out of room in the foyer, the kids hung their art on the wall down the hall toward the art room itself, which was large and open and had a beautiful glass cherub's head set high in a transom above the door. Anna herself had drawn another picture, this time of the statue outside of the school, the one with the man supporting the two other soldiers. There were little hatch marks in the man's coat, and up close you could see that Anna had tried, in small pen-and-ink letters, to write the names of the soldiers that were engraved on the statue itself. She hung the picture now beside the art room door.

Anna really was talented, thought Bett grudgingly. Who'd've thought she'd even pay attention to that kind of thing?

"You guys," Anna was telling her friends as she trimmed the paper around her piece with an X-Acto knife, "I found the best YouTube channel." But Bett was focused on Mutt, who was looking closely at Anna's picture.

"You got my dad's name on there," he said to Anna. "Good."

"Glad you care," said Anna.

Mutt didn't respond. But he pulled a folded piece of paper out of his back pocket and taped it to the wall beside Anna's picture. Mutt's work was nothing beautiful. It was pure Mutt, a picture of a stuffed rabbit impaled on a tree with a sword. There was blood coming out of the bunny, even though it was clearly a toy. Disturbing in the extreme.

"What the eff?" Bett asked Mutt.

Mutt shrugged. "It's just a picture."

"Dillhole," muttered Bett. Lucky her, she was going to get to spend the afternoon with Mutt again for cross-country.

"What do you think?" asked Dan, who came to stand next to her.

"Did Ranger bring in a picture?" Bett asked him.

Dan laughed. "No way," he said. "The art gene missed us both by a mile. That's why he spends all his time inventing new stupid shit to say."

"Cakes," Bett couldn't help adding, and Dan play socked her in the arm. Bett stepped back.

"I brought one, though," said Dan. "There's this cheese-burger I draw. And a sun—with sunglasses."

Bett stared at him. "You have been drawing those since we were in fourth grade," she said. "Mr. Thorne was always after you."

"I know!" said Dan happily, and he taped up his burger.

"We are going to plaster this place with art," Anna was saying now. "And who cares if that bastard slashes every single one. We'll just bring more. Fists together!" And the whole group put its fists together, except Bett, because she was certainly not a part of this.

But then Anna called out, "Come on, Bett!" Bett shook her head. "You're a supporter," Anna encouraged her, but Bett could only make a throat gargle noise and stepped farther back. Anna's shoulders dropped. Then there was a great show of everybody bumping everybody else's fists, shouting, "ART LEAGUE!" at the top of their lungs.

It was a bit too much togetherness for Bett, but the art part was kind of cool. She had to give them that.

28

Wednesday,
Day Five of Eleventh Grade

"LET'S SIT OUTSIDE AT LUNCH," SAID PAUL IN ENGLISH class. Did he mean Bett, too, or just the other kids at the table? She didn't want to look like a loser who thought she belonged where she didn't. Besides, lunch with Hester was not high on Bett's list of priorities. Still, it was a beautiful day, she had to admit, and while sitting outside was a privilege open to upperclassmen, Bett had not yet taken part because she was afraid being outside would start a chain reaction of Plus thoughts like walking then running then racing until she was panting with exhaustion and she had to fight that kind of impulse, fight it harder than ever.

But nonetheless, at lunch Bett found herself trailing behind the group with her tray to sit on the steps of the school. She sat by the statue, just far enough away that the other kids could ignore her if they hadn't meant for her to join them, and also so she could look like she didn't consider herself a part of them, either.

Bett reached out and fingered the coat of the man in the statue. She was sore from yesterday's forced run. Even her arms hurt as she stretched them toward the hem of the bronzed jacket. There was a grackle on each of the man's shoulders, but, surprisingly, they didn't fly away at her gesture. More interested in the possibility of crumbs from her hot dog buns, Bett imagined. Her fingers ran over some of the names of the veterans on the coat, carved in so skillfully they just looked like part of the wrinkles and falls of the man's jacket and the clothes of the men he was bearing. Bett hadn't thought about those names in a while, not before Anna's drawing had drawn her attention to them again.

Now Dan came clattering outside and sat beside her in the space she had left between herself and the group. She dropped her hand from the man's coat.

Dan read her thoughts. "Think of the ones who were killed," he said. "Can you imagine? Men and women in our town who would be, like, full adults now with work and families and stuff."

"Maybe divorced and bored of their jobs and closeted, too," said Paul.

"You're ghoulish, Paul," said Dan. "It's a waste and . . . sad."

For the Stays, thought Bett. Twinklers didn't enlist nearly as often.

Paul shrugged. "It was cool of Anna to include some of the names on her picture. Damn, that girl has talent."

Dan nodded. "More than I ever could have," he said.

Bett took a deep breath and steadied her voice. "Me either," she said finally. "But I think it's good you guys are doing this."

"Anna's idea," said Dan.

Above Bett's head, the grackle on the man's right shoulder flew away at last. She thought about Ranger and his wild gesticulations with his friends. He was up to something. She had to tell Dan.

"Listen," Bett said to Dan, lowering her voice a little. "I'm kind of worried about your brother."

"Ranger?" said Dan, cocking his head. "He's the last kid you have to worry about. He's, like, almost clinically happy. The only thing you have to worry about with him is that he might irritate the hell out of someone with his 'cakes' and wind up the victim of a swirly." He looked at Bett. "Your bangs look nice like that."

Bett shrugged and shook her head at the same time. What to say to that without sounding like she thought she looked nice, too?

"I don't mean Ranger getting teased," she said at last. "Ranger and his friends were running around inside the school the other day and talking at lunch like little maniacs. I think they're *investigating* the fire slashing and the devil pictures. They're racing around making theories and stuff."

Dan was quiet. Then: "Sounds like the little jerk."

"Well, I'm worried—whoever attacked the art must have brought a box cutter to school—"

"Or an X-Acto knife," added Paul. Bett glanced over at him. Since when did Paul pay any attention to what Bett was saying? Huh.

But she continued. "And slashed the hell out of those drawings—I don't want your brother in any danger."

Dan shrugged, but then he went still. "Okay. You're right. I'll keep an eye on the kid."

"I will, too," said Bett. "Just to make sure he doesn't detect the person and try to march them to the main office himself."

Dan laughed, but Bett knew he was concerned because his face stayed serious. "Thanks," he said.

Bett squirmed and said nothing.

Luckily, Paul added, "I'm with you both on this one."

But they were interrupted by Anna running out of the school, frantic. "It happened again!" she yelled, fists clenched. "Again!"

Immediately, she was mobbed by kids.

"The art again?" everyone was asking—at least everybody who hadn't abandoned their lunch trays to race inside to the foyer to see for themselves.

"YES!" Anna cried. "My wings! Our work we brought in this morning!"

Bett ran with everyone else back into the school. Green and blue and red paper feathers lay everywhere on the floor. Ripped and shredded to bits, along with torn pictures and shadow boxes smashed. And above the carnage of the wings, above the blue-green burn-curled scraps still stuck to the wall, spray-painted words on the tiles screamed:

I'M GOING TO GUT THIS PLACE.

"Oh my God!" cried Hester. "What kind of asshole would do all this?"

Paul was incredulous. "And why? Why?"

Bett looked at those artworks slashed and smashed into shreds and shards all over the floor, and as awful as it was, she shivered, not because of the horror of it, but because all she could imagine was what it must have felt like, smashing things and slashing those wings. It must have felt like punching the river. Like being free.

29

Wednesday,
Day Five of Eleventh Grade

AFTER SCHOOL, MUTT, DAN, RANGER, AND BETT headed to the bus to be taken to I Know a Guy Field. Behind them, on Salt River K–12's actual athletic grounds, the field hockey team was practicing with their sticks, passing small balls to one another down the field. A shot went wild; the ball went high, and Hester shouted, "Incoming!"

Eddie dropped to the ground with a *thud*.

There was a pause.

"You okay?" asked Dan, puzzled.

But Bett knew. "Reaction," she said. "You want a hand up?"

"Shut up," suggested Eddie. His face was redder than ever and his baseball hat was askew. "Around for enough grenades, there's consequences when a man hears a word like that."

They watched him struggle painfully to his feet.

"Get the hell on my bus," he told them.

They got the hell on his bus.

Bett was so sore from yesterday's practice she couldn't even consider reaching down to touch her toes when Eddie shouted out the command.

"Second day is always the worst," Mutt told them. "Your muscles aren't accustomed to being used again yet."

They're not used to being scared witless by a psycho with an art vengeance, either, Bett thought. Her heart was still beating hard from what they'd seen in the foyer. Once was freaky enough. But twice . . . twice was another whole level of scary.

Think about something else, she ordered herself. Like since when was Mutt an athletic instructor? Bett couldn't shake her junior high image of him, out of breath during basketball games, passing the ball wildly away from himself whenever anyone passed to him.

He must have wanted to get better, Bett realized. *He is a good runner now. That can't have come easy.* Bett had to give Mutt credit for having had a goal to improve even though he was still a complete homophobic buttwipe.

"You touch those toes," Eddie warned her.

"Yeah," said Mutt.

Shut up, Mutt.

"And don't make me get in my bus today," said Eddie.

"Nobody *makes* you get in that bus," Bett said back, borderline sass, even though she did feel bad for Eddie, dropping to the ground like that. What must it be like to have been in a war, a real war, and have live grenades come at you? Things Bett remembered her father telling her about the Vietnam War came to her, like how the Vietnam War vets had come home to everyone being mad at them for having even gone to fight in the first place when it wasn't their fault.

"My plan is to stay in this I Know a Guy Field," she muttered now, touching her toes.

Ranger glanced over at her. "You aren't the only one with a plan," he said, making his voice low and mysterious.

"Some plans are safer than others," Dan started, pegging Ranger with a look as they stood back up.

But Eddie interrupted.

"If you think I can't chase you around this field, Bett, you got another think coming." The vision of Eddie in the bus, weaving behind her as she tried to zigzag out of his way filled Bett's mind. She wouldn't put it past him, not after yesterday's practice and not after his just having dropped to the ground a few minutes ago, freaked out by a field hockey ball.

So she touched her toes again. She couldn't stop thinking again about the ruined wings and art. And the graffiti took it beyond the pale. That was some terrifying shit. The destruction, the devils, all of it.

Who would destroy things like that? And *why*?

Other than that wonderful feeling.

No. Shut up about that.

Bett had enough to worry about without being a perp sympathizer, because not only did her bangs look kickass, she was about to have another afternoon of Plus-running the cross-country practice course. Thinking about her bangs reminded her of her lunchtime blush at Dan's compliment, which made her worry she would blush again about it now, but at least if she was red here on the field it would look exercise related. Why did she have to blush so much around Dan?

"Two laps around the field," said Mutt, stupid clipboard in his hand. "Then the same loop as yesterday, only turn and head back here after you hit Ridge Road."

"Boring," said Ranger. "Can't we add distance some other way?"

"No," said Mutt.

"Don't question my plan," said Eddie. "I can chase you with the bus, too. Now run." He gave Bett a look. "All of you."

Whatever. Bett ran. But not before she had stolen Mutt's pen off his clipboard and written BURN on the bottom of her sole.

Running. Ground pacing under her feet, speed increasing, breathing harder, muscles aching, and all of it too amazing. The nervejangle inside her head was partly undoing the pleasure, though, which Bett was glad about, because then maybe she wouldn't have to punish herself so hard later.

"Move it," Mutt groused at them as practice ended and they made their way back to the bus. "I gotta get home to watch my sister."

"You have a sister?" asked Ranger, surprised.

"Yeah," said Mutt. "She's eight, so I have to be there when she gets home from being at her friend's house and shit." He disappeared into the bus.

"Bett!" Eddie shouted plaintively after her when the boys were all on the bus. "Come here!" He paused. "I want to *talk* to you!"

Bett stopped short. "NO!" she shouted. "You promised!" And she ran away from the bus and back across the field, faster than she had run the whole course today.

"Bett!"

Shut up! Bett screamed in her head. *Don't you think I already know I'm a thousand times worse than a wings destroyer?*

Crows were pecking their way among the grass and pebbles when Bett reached the opposite edge of the field. The ones to her left all flew away at her approach.

30

Wednesday,
After Day Five of Eleventh Grade

WALKING TOWARD THE SLOPE TO THE SHACK AFTER the bus ride home from cross-country, Bett's phone buzzed. It was a text from her dad.

I miss you, it said. **Please call.**

Bett would not call. She did not call her dad, she did not go to visit him, even though he, Bill, Stephanie, and Stephanie's mother had moved, too, two years ago, sold the Christmas tree farm, which was all grown over now and towering with too-tall trees. They lived just in the next town now. All her father's texting and e-mailing and Bett would have none of that, either, she barely spoke to him when he called her on the landline her mom had had to put in because the little spit of land where the house shack sat did not have reliable cell service, not yet, anyway, through

189

the summer and early fall, when there were so many leaves on the trees surrounding the path up the slope. At least that's what they were hoping the reason was. But the front of the house was nothing but those grasses, and sometimes Bett's phone worked there.

Why does he keep trying? Why doesn't he realize he's an asswipe who does not deserve to talk to his own kid, the one he didn't even bother to check on after the explosion (good old Bett, good old strong-boned Bett, she can take care of herself), the one he—

She deleted the text but the familiar tide was overtaking her. She gave her head a shake. *Please don't go on with that train of thought. Please.* And it stopped as, shifting her heavy backpack until she reached the SIM card house, Bett checked the river for the man.

He wasn't there.

She was surprised to find herself disappointed. What was it about him that made her hope to see him, somehow? She thought of his strong arms, casting and fishing, and wished again he were here to see now.

Mom wasn't in the house when Bett went inside, but Aunt Jeanette was. "You should have one of those crates on wheels," Aunt Jeanette said critically. "That knapsack is shit for your back."

Could you imagine? Going to high school with a crate on wheels like a stewardess or, even worse, a teacher?

"I'm fine," said Bett. "How are you? How was work?"

"I'm just trying to prevent you from becoming a stooped-over old woman," Aunt Jeanette said. "But if you turn out that way, don't come crying to me!"

"If I turn out that way, you'll be laughing as I change your diapers anyway," said Bett, and Aunt Jeanette made a face as the landline rang.

"Don't answer it!" But Bett was already too late and after a brief "How's the Floozy?" Aunt Jeanette handed the phone to Bett.

Bett held it and was silent.

"Bett?"

Who else would be breathing over here in her own house?

"Bett, please, honey. I love you. Stephanie—"

Bett hung up and went to her room, half poised to escape. But she heard her mother come in in a whirl of grocery bags, her mom and Aunt Jeanette talking and talking and talking.

"So guess what the construction jagweed story part two turns out to be," said Aunt Jeanette. Bett could tell she was dying to tell Bett's mother that Bett's dad had phoned and she had called him out about the Floozy, but she wouldn't dare right now, not in this tiny shack of a house with Bett four stairs up in a room the size of a teleporter.

"He called the owner of the company," said Aunt Jeanette. "And the owner told him to go eff himself. How's that for justice?"

"Karma's a bitch," said Bett's mom.

"I hate when people say that," said Aunt Jeanette with surprising vehemence. "What karma? Who gets punished for the bullshit they do? Ted with the Floozy and Bett with her ear. Who got punished for all that?"

"Bett," said her mother, hoisting something big into the fridge, from the sound of it.

"Tell me about it!" said Aunt Jeanette. "She has not one friend anymore. She won't even *talk* to a girl her own age. How is that karma fair?"

"It's not karma," said Bett's mom, sounding tired. Over the police radio in the kitchen came a crackly voice.

"Domestic disturbance on Field Road," it said. "Marianne, you available?"

"YES!" Bett's mother shouted. Then, very softly but Bett could still hear: "Jeanette. Bett isn't friends with girls anymore because she's afraid she'll kill them."

31

Wednesday Late Afternoon, Still

THAT IS NOT WHY! THAT IS NOT! I'M NOT FRIENDS WITH girls because they hate me.

That's not true.

Insistent as a cat, the thought came into her mind and Bett couldn't take it. She knew her mother was right. After the explosion—so many girls inviting her over, asking her to eat lunch with them, hang with them, but Bett always said no until they stopped trying. But so what. She was fine, and besides, Stephanie was alive, not dead, no matter what Midnight Bett's mind and its hidden Tastykakes believed, which was stupid and she knew it, but it was hard to shake that thought, either. The only thing that could shake it was eating and not dreaming about Fizzicle Feets, but even that was getting messed up because everything was getting too

Plus now with the way she was all turned around with this stupid cross-country team and being chased by buses and dreams of climbing up the rope in gym class instead of sitting like a lump against the wall and her mother knowing the truth and what if Bett killed someone else?

Else?

No.

Just someone. Stephanie may not be dead, but Bett knew she was dead to Stephanie. Missing her right eye because of Bett, for God's sake. Who would let a person like that stay alive in her mind?

What else could she take away from herself? Bett had learned to be still, and now she had a madman with a bus shaking her into motion—more than motion. Action with danger and talking to people. What was she going to do? Her left ear dimmed as her hunger grew.

32

TWO YEARS AGO . . . Living in the house they had lived in with her father was hell. Bett and her mother hated it silently, each knowing the other felt the same way. At first Bett hoped they would move right away so she wouldn't have to see her father's crap stuff and smell his crap smell. But then she decided it was only what she deserved.

The first few months helped because of the not-hearing part. Bett's right ear recovered first. It was bizarre, because the world went from muted nothing to too loud almost overnight. Everyone else was ecstatic, of course. Bett could hear! She was healing!

"Now she'll get back to being herself," Aunt Jeanette kept saying.

But Bett would never get back to being herself.

It was slow, realizing all the things she didn't deserve. Obviously, no Fizzicle Feets. No running. No doing anything that might make her muscles feel used or her pent-up feeling released. Then no letting herself think about anything to do with moving, even, not any part of her body. She did not deserve to. She didn't deserve a thing. All she knew was her sole on that hose and she didn't deserve a thing. Only to live in this hell house of memory and her dad's shoes and make herself remember, every day, what she had done, what she was capable of doing.

33

Thursday Morning,
Day Six of Eleventh Grade

THIS MORNING BETT WASHED HER HAIR AND DID HER bangs. Then she hesitated.

Why not? Who said she had to wear her hair up every day? For practice, maybe, but not in the day. She got the blow-dryer back out and blew her long hair dry, too, letting it wave and curve like ribbons down her back.

It's not like anyone looks at my head anyway.

But by the time Eddie pulled up, Bett's hair was back in the messy topknot, although her bangs still looked kick-ass. Someday, though. Maybe.

"The perp *must* be tallcakes," said Ranger on the bus.

"Ranger, quit being a detective about this whole thing," said Dan.

Ranger was startled. "How did you know?"

"Only maybe you talking about perps and your little posse racing around like madmen," said Dan. "We all know. And you *should* quit it, because the perp, as you say, is probably insane, and you are not, like, physically safe pursuing them."

"But I've been coming up with more theories since last night," said Ranger. "They must be tallcakes because a lot of that art was hung up highcakes."

"Ranger, the perp could have just stood on a chair," Bett couldn't help herself from pointing out.

Ranger was silent. Then: "Maybe there are two of them!" he cried, positively glowing. "One tall, and one short, and the tall one hoisted the short onecakes! I like detecting."

"*Ranger*," said Dan, and Bett could tell he was at his wits' end. Ranger was tenacious, and plus, the "cakes" thing was really getting legs, and Bett knew it was driving Dan crazy. Bett still kind of loved it. *Why?* she wondered, but then she knew. She loved focus and single-mindedness, and Ranger had both in spades. *Yay, Ranger.* But even so:

"Ranger," said Bett. "Be careful. You don't know what kind of person this is."

"Yes, I do," said Ranger. "I just said. A tall one. Maybe with a short friend."

Undivertable. Still, though, who could it be? Who hated the school or Salt River so much they'd do these things? Besides Bett?

Stop.

"You kids better take it easy today," said Eddie. "I got quite a plan for your workout this afternoon."

"He's not kidding," Mutt added.

"I got quite a plan, too," muttered Ranger, just as he had yesterday.

Bett's phone buzzed, and she took it out of her bag, one eye on Eddie in the mirror in case he noticed.

**I can't get Ranger off this. Help me. He likes you.
He'll listen to you if you tell him to quit it with
this BS.**

It was from Dan. Bett's eyes went wide. How did he even have her number? How did she have his? Oh, yeah. That ninth-grade Social Studies project. He'd kept her number since then? Bett texted back:

**I'll try. But I don't know how to get him away from
it without scaring him.**

Maybe that's the way to go.

"Who are you texting?" asked Ranger in his clear, high voice.

"WHAT!" Eddie slammed on the brakes, but this time Bett was ready for him and she put a hand against the seat in front of her to minimize impact. "Who! Who's texting on my bus?"

There was silence. "Me," said Bett finally.

"And me," said Dan.

"Well, that's it," said Eddie, grinding the bus into gear again. Mutt just shook his head by the window. "I'm writing you two bozos up."

"We're sorry, Eddie!" said Dan. "Don't write us up. We won't do it again, will we, Bett?"

"Promise," said Bett. "Please, Eddie. Detention is so boring."

"And besides," said Dan, "if we're in detention we can't come to cross-country practice, and it's just you and Ranger and the grim reaper over there."

"Shut up," said Mutt.

"You are not to disrespect the rules on my bus," said Eddie. "You want me to throw your phones?" And it was true they were at the row of basement holes again.

"No," said Bett and Dan together.

"Then I'm writing you up. Insubordination."

34

Still Thursday,
Day Six of Eleventh Grade

WHEN THEY WALKED INTO THE SCHOOL, THE AIR WAS charged and electric, and not just because the graffiti had been washed off the wall where Anna's wings had hung. A few kids were standing by the ghost of the letters still left on the wall, but most everyone else was gathered around the art room door, looking down, then up, then down again.

Bett chose down. The floor was pebbled with broken glass.

"What the hell?"

"AGAIN?"

"What's going on?" Dan asked as he approached the group.

"The cherub!" Anna cried. "The cherub was smashed!"

"What cherub?" Dan looked puzzled. Bett looked up. *What the HELL?*

"The one that was over the art room door!" Anna pointed up at the transom. And indeed, where the cherub had just yesterday faced into the hallway, there was nothing now but the wood of the transom frame edged with broken glass. "I need a broom," Anna said, and a kid took off for the janitor's closet. "I'm keeping all this." She waved her hand out over the shards.

"What for?" Paul asked.

But Anna was too distracted to answer. The kid returned with the broom, and Anna began gently sweeping up the glass.

The din grew louder as Mr. McLean came around the corner.

"Everybody back," he said loudly. "Anna! Stop that! That glass is evidence!"

"Who cares!" cried Anna. "You're not going to find fingerprints on pulverized glass!"

"In my office! Now!"

The other kids roared in protest. But Bett looked down at the floor again. There was dirt—a lot of it. She left the group yelling at Mr. McLean as he led Anna down the hall, and followed the dirt along the floor in the opposite direction, up the stairs to the second-floor landing.

A dirt path.

Bett thought about it. Hard.

35

Thursday,
Day Six of Eleventh Grade

ANNA PASSED BETT AND DAN COMING INTO THE OFFICE as she was heading out of it.

"What'd he give you?" Dan asked her.

Anna rolled her eyes. "Detention. But I don't care. I have the glass." And she let the office door bang shut behind her.

"You're up," said Mrs. Schlovsky to Bett and Dan, and they headed into Mr. McLean's inner office.

"What's this I hear about you two kids being insubordinate to the bus driver?" Mr. McLean was one of the hairiest men Bett had ever seen. He had a mustache and a beard, so much beard, in fact, that you could tell he just made a decision to shave a certain part of his neck so it wouldn't count as chest hair as well.

"We texted," said Bett. Might as well come clean.

"Why?" asked Mr. McLean.

"Um," said Dan.

"We had . . ." Bett swallowed. "We had stuff to say."

"Well," said the principal, "why don't you say it out loud right now?"

Bett looked at him. The principal looked at her. Bett won. He looked away first.

"Detention," he said. "This afternoon. Not smart, kids. This is junior year. It'll go onto the records we send to your college choices."

Dan gulped.

"Can we go?" asked Bett.

"When I say you can," said Mr. McLean evenly. "How about this . . . this destruction around the school? You two know anything about that?"

"No," said Bett. Dan said nothing and Bett knew he was thinking of Ranger.

She was right.

"Do you all, like, have any leads?" Dan asked Mr. McLean finally. "I'm worried about kids trying to track this psycho down themselves and getting hurt."

"Who?" asked Mr. McLean sharply. "Who are you worried about?"

"No one in particular," said Dan hastily.

"We take this very seriously," said Mr. McLean. "Destruction of school property is a serious offense. Not to mention hate speech on the walls. If you have any information, we need to know."

"I don't," said Dan.

There was a silence.

Then: "Now may we go?" Dan asked.

"Please do," said Mr. McLean, and Bett was aware of Mr. McLean's eyes on their backs as they left.

"I've never had detention," said Dan. "Can you do homework?"

"No," said Bett. "You can only sit." She dreaded it. She knew the forced stillness would only make her brain churn faster.

But Dan was clutching at his hair, and it stuck up at all angles, so she said, "It's really no biggie. And no more of a pain in the ass than cross-country is. Same amount of time until we take the late bus home. With Eddie."

"But I'm supposed to . . ."

Dan trailed off, and Bett knew what he meant. He was supposed to keep an eye on Ranger, and Ranger needed that eye on him.

36

Autumn, Still the Endless Sixth Day
of Eleventh Grade

ART WAS THIRD PERIOD TODAY, AND ONCE AGAIN, AS Bett approached, there was a crowd around the door, necks craned upward this time.

Oh, no. Not more crap destroyed!

But it wasn't that.

Hanging from the ceiling was an explosion of light: shards of glass painted gold and silver and glowing like a star, a mobile shining like a vehicle for a god. Anna. She had taken the shards of glass from the cherub and made this. She must have skipped her first two classes to do it, McLean and his detention notwithstanding.

"Jesus," said Mutt. "When is she going to stop making stuff out of the crap getting busted?"

"Never," said Anna, whirling around to face him. "I

will never stop." And, standing on one of the art room stools, she reached up with her thin hands and anchored the sculpture more firmly in place over the empty transom.

Bett's heart beat loud as a drum. She was surprised Anna couldn't hear it.

Dan was in this class with her. So was Doug. Fabulous.

Anna walked up to Dan and sat down next to him, looking shaky. He put his arm around her.

"Your piece is gorgeous," he told her.

"It is," Bett added. *There. I can, too, talk to girls. Take that, Aunt Jeanette.*

"Thank you," said Anna. "That's nice of you."

"It's true," Dan insisted. "How did you do all that without cutting yourself to ribbons?"

"I did get cut to ribbons," Anna admitted, showing her hands to him. They were covered in tiny cuts.

Stop it this minute, Bett told herself, hand over her wrist.

"I can't stand that you can still see those horrible graffiti words on the walls by where my wings used to be," Anna said.

"They're scary hateful," Bett started to say, but now Mr. Thorne, the art teacher, was talking.

"That angel head over the transom was blown glass," he announced. "Made by a student here in the nineties who survived an IED explosion in the Gulf War but ultimately died of his wounds after he came home. He made that when he was in tenth grade, before the war, when we still had glass-blowing equipment here."

The room was quiet. "Is his name on the soldier's coat outside?" asked Anna finally.

"Yup," said Mr. Thorne. "Michael Lorde." He lowered his head a moment. "Good kid," he said finally, looking back up at them. "Anna, I love what you made. If anyone gives you trouble for making it, tell them to see me." He shook his head. "Okay, you all. Let's get started. This was going to be the start of our clay unit, but you should feel free to make it a free draw period instead if that suits you better."

"Can I say something first, Mr. Thorne?" asked Anna.

"Sure," said the teacher.

Anna stood up. "A lot of you know this already," she said, "but some of us have formed a group to kind of, like, stand up to whatever crazy person this is, wrecking the art. We're having a meeting tonight. If you want to come, see me or Eli Gonzales. We'll give you more details then."

"I think that's great, Anna," said Mr. Thorne. "Keep fighting destruction with creation."

"That's pretty much the idea," said Anna, and sat down again. Then everyone got busy drawing, rain slanting against the windows.

At least Dan and I won't have to run in that wetness, thought Bett. *What with detention and all.*

Dan took up a pencil and began to draw his sun. Bett watched.

"Why don't you draw something?" Dan asked her, making a careful layer of sunbeams.

"I don't draw," said Bett.

"You must be able to draw something," said Dan. "You were, like, so good with your makeup." This time he was the one who looked away.

"I could only draw on my own face," she said, trying to keep the surprise from showing. "And it was pretty much the same every time."

"So are my sun and my cheeseburger," Dan pointed out.

"I think I'll get some clay." Bett went over to the clay bucket sitting at the bottom of the shelves Mr. Thorne used for works-in-progress for the little kids. On the lowest shelf were rows of tiny goblets. Most were endearingly awkward and clunky, with hearts etched on them or skulls. One was particularly lovely, though, smooth, with three snakey, pointy swirls curling around themselves on the clay. Bett reached out a finger to trace them.

MRS. LEDGER'S GRADE 3, the sign next to them said. NORSE UNIT.

But before she could think any more about the goblets:

"FUCK!" Across the room Doug was standing up, holding a piece of paper in his hand.

"Don't you dare swear in here!" said Mr. Thorne.

"Look at this!" Doug yelled. "It was in my pocket! Look!"

He held up the paper so everyone could see. There was no mistaking it. It was another one of those devil pictures, horned and terrifying.

In Doug's pocket? In his *pocket*? In Doug's pocket meant . . . meant that the art psycho had been near enough to a person to actually plant a picture on him, in his clothes, without him knowing!

"It's a death threat!" someone cried.

"Shut up!" Doug threw the paper on the floor and kicked it away.

"What the hell is going on?" someone else said, voice wavering.

"Calm down, everyone, calm down," the art teacher said, holding his hands up as if to soothe their thoughts. But he was clearly freaked out, too. "Doug, hand me that paper. I'm going to turn it over to the principal. I think it's time for us to step things up another notch."

Despite her hatred of Doug, Bett found her arms were goose-bumping. Whoever was doing this wasn't playing.

For once, she was glad her mother was involved.

37

Autumn, Thursday, Sixth Day
of this Weirdass Eleventh Grade Year

"THAT WAS TOTALLY CREEPY," DAN SAID AS THEY LEFT art class.

"No kidding," said Bett. She found herself eyeballing every kid they walked by. One of them was doing this, and it felt like it was leading up to a kid in the news who went crazy and then shot everyone at school. Bett had a serious, petrified pit in her stomach. That bomb threat last year—who was it? The same nut? Why hadn't her mother been able to find that one? Maybe her mother was as shitty a detective as Ranger.

But Bett knew that wasn't true. It was more to do with the tiny size of the Salt River Police Department, and the fact that her mother was one-third of it. Sometimes the surrounding small towns teamed up for stuff, but that cost money, and none of the towns really had any. Still. Bett wished she had talked to her mother about the devil heads the first time they had appeared. What was her mother thinking about all this? Bett wished she would spill a theory or two. It would be comforting, somehow, if her mom had a lead.

Dan sat with Bett at lunch, along with Paul and, surprisingly, Ranger.

"Where's your posse?" she asked him as he plunked his tray down. Two chocolate milks. Kids.

"In trouble," said Ranger morosely. "They didn't do their math homework, so they had to go back to math for lunch."

"That stinks." Bett tried to smile reassuringly. He looked a little nervous. Not from eating with bigger kids— Ranger never seemed to notice he was out of place in these situations—but because of something else, and Bett had a hunch it had to do with the art.

"Are you scared about the drawings and the devils?" she whispered when everyone was talking with everyone else.

"No," said Ranger quickly. "Well, I'm kinda scared because I think I should've kept my mouth shut better about investigating. But it wasn't just me. Joaquin bragged when we were in Social Studies, and now he and Martin are both in trouble for math, and they both like Ms. Sparrow, so what if they tell her and adults get involved and I get clobbered by the perp?"

Poor Ranger.

But that wasn't even the half of it, as it turned out.

The second lunch bell rang, and in came a swoop of upperclassmen, all of them agitated as a guy named Sam was yelping, only with his huge self, even a yelp sounded deep. "What the hell?!" He took a paper out of his own pocket and slammed what was clearly another devil drawing onto the table. It wafted to the floor. "Check this out. What's next, a guy with a gun?"

Bett's heart sped up. Guys like Sam never let on that they were scared. And Sam was scared.

"Hell no," boomed Doug, calmer for sure than when he'd found his own drawing, or at least fronting it. "I am going to find this asshole and beat the shit out of them. No one threatens The Doug. No one."

"The Doug," muttered Bett.

"Psst, Bett . . ." It was Dan. "I'm thinking maybe we should go to Anna's meeting tonight. We need to make a plan."

"Yeah!" Ranger chimed in. "Let's make a good plan!"

"We don't mean you, idiot," said Dan. "Older heads are going to prevail here."

"What older heads? Your older head is stupidcakes," said Ranger, looking stung.

Bett and Dan exchanged glances. "Only upperclassmen are invited," Bett said soothingly.

"Are you planning on more art? To show the perp you aren't scared?" asked Ranger. "Because I can draw."

Dan shook his head. "Kid, you are no artist," he said.

Now Ranger was enraged. "I can, too, draw!" he insisted. And he picked up a Sharpie and started drawing on a wrinkled piece of paper fished from his backpack.

"I gotta stay at your house again Columbus Day weekend," Mutt was telling one of his minions at the table behind them.

"Why?"

"My mom is going to Ohio or something. Some new guy. My dad'll be away, too. Car conference. You think your sister would be cool with my sister coming, too?"

But Bett couldn't focus on Mutt, not while she watched Ranger. What was up with that picture? He was drawing a silly sheep-looking thing, but something about it was familiar to Bett.

It wasn't until Ranger drew the awkward devil horns on his weird little sheep thing that—No. No! But yes. Bett knew.

Ranger was the devil-drawer.

38

Thursday, Day Six of Eleventh Grade, Lunch

IT HIT DAN AT THE SAME TIME. "NO WAY—NO WAY!" HE said, leaping up. Bett grabbed Ranger's picture. What were they going to do? No wonder Ranger was so skittish, so nervous. He was the . . . but . . . but . . . Ranger? Rangercakes? Bett looked again at the drawing. There was no doubt. Arrgh! What the hell was going on? Her brain raced. The stupid drawings were definitely Ranger, but the drawing slashing and burning and the graffiti and angel smashing? Bett's brain was churning, thinking back. Ranger *could* have attacked those drawings when he left the caf that first day to "go to the bathroom," and he probably tried to cover up his guilt by calling all of the lunch-eaters to come see what he himself had really done. *Oh my God.*

She jumped up.

"What's the matter?" asked Paul, startled.

"I forgot to take Ranger to the nurse . . . for his medicine!" cried Bett. "Come on, Ranger!"

Paul cocked his head. "Isn't he old enough to take himself to the nurse?"

"Uh—" Bett started, even as Ranger piped up, "I don't have to go to the nurse," and Dan punched him and said, "Yes, you do."

They had to get him alone. Find out exactly what he and his tiny terrorist group were up to, and Bett was going to have to stop them, and her mother would be even more involved, never mind Mr. McLean, and this was all so much more horrible than if the slasher-crasher person was a stranger. And he'd wind up in juvie—Ranger!

The second they got into the hallway, Dan lit into him. "You goddamn idiot, you drew those devil drawings, didn't you!" he spat out, punching Ranger in the arm. "Those horns are a dead giveaway!"

Ranger's eyes were wide. "It wasn't me! I swear!"

Dan looked apoplectic. "Of course it was you." His voice tight, dangerous. "You can't draw, man, and everything you can't draw is can't-drawn the same way." He shook Ranger's arm, hard. "Spill it!"

"I didn't ruin those summer pictures," Ranger pleaded, his voice tight and high-pitched. "Honest to God I didn't! And I didn't mess up the wings or smash the cherub or write that graffiti message either!"

"No?" Dan's face was now an inch from his brother's. "You just thought devil heads would accentuate them all nicely?"

Ranger choked out a sob. Bett felt bad, even if he might be a baby psycho.

"Okay! I did do the drawings," Ranger confessed at last. "But that's all! It isn't like you think. I didn't do those other things! Everybody will think I did those other things!"

Bett looked around nervously. "We better go outside. I don't like talking in the halls like this."

"I can't," Ranger wailed. "I'm not an upperclassman!"

"Just come," said Dan, grabbing him by the upper arm. "We'll say you're with us."

"We'll figure this out, Ranger," Bett assured him, even though she was in no way sure. Ranger snuffled. Bett lowered her voice. "Explain to us exactly what you did do and why, and maybe we can help you."

"Or get Bett's mom to arrest you," muttered Dan, and Ranger was crying, and Bett gave Dan a *cool it* look. Hard.

Outside, the rain had stopped, but the air was still damp.

Ranger was now in full sobbing, gulping mode. "Those drawings aren't even devils," he hiccupped out. "They're about justice."

"Dude, they're devils," said Dan. "Look." He pulled out the picture Sam had dropped, and there it was, the same devil blowing flames.

N. GRIFFIN

"It's not a *devil*," Ranger insisted. "It's *justice*."

"What the hell are you on about?" asked Dan.

"Me and my friends knew we couldn't take on the art destroyer. But we wanted them to know we were watching them. So we made up a symbol of justice to leave at the crime scenes."

Bett gaped at him. "Your symbol of justice was a devil?"

"It's not! I keep telling you! It's a—"

"A what?" Dan demanded.

Ranger turned beet red. "A tufty-eared mountain lion of justice. Breathing out justice in a big breath cloud."

"Breathing out justice in a big breath cloud?" Bett and Dan said in unison.

"Yes," said Ranger. His tears had slowed.

"So," said Bett, aiming for calm. "You drew a mountain lion, not a devil. To . . . scare? Yes?"—Ranger nodded—"The person doing all this wack destruction. Is that it?"

"Yes," Ranger said again. "Cakes," he added.

"Dammit, Ranger!" Dan was beside himself. "Don't you know the minute you draw anything else the game is up?"

"He won't draw a thing from now on," said Bett. "At least, not for a while. Right, Ranger?"

"Ranger, you are a nutjob," said Dan. "Nobody would ever guess those pictures are about *justice*, and if anyone suspects it was you—"

"I know!" cried Ranger. "And my fingerprints are all over the walls and the tufty-eared-mountain-lion pictures,

218

too! And . . . and . . . Eddie knows I have those plastic knives sometimes to peel my apples with! What if they ask him if I had one the day the pictures were slashed? Why didn't I wear gloves?" His eyes brimmed with tears again.

"Don't worry about that, Ranger," said Bett. "Without your prints already on file, the police won't know it's you. Unless you do something else stupid and get caught and my mom takes your prints for that. Then you're screwed."

"I won't!" cried Ranger. "And I'll never draw my mountain lion again!" Then he frowned. "What'll I do in art class, though?"

"What the hell, Ranger?" Dan exploded. "Who cares about art class? Listen, douche, if anyone else makes the connection between your other stupid artwork and . . . this tufty-eared devil of righteousness or whatever, they are going to think you are the one who destroyed school property and threatened the school, and you, my brother, are in for it. On top of that, Mom and Dad will kill you. The principal will kill you. Bett's mother will probably kill you. You are totally dead."

"So what do I do?" Ranger wept, head bowed. "And what if the psycho finds out it's me?"

But there was something Bett wanted to know. "How did you hide those pictures in people's clothes?" she asked.

Ranger's head shot up. "I have study hall first period. Me and the guys asked to go to the library and we just went to the boys' locker room in the gym instead."

"But why the boys' locker room?"

"No one ever really locks their lockers," Ranger explained, "so we could go in and put the pictures in people's pockets. We targeted the tallest guys first. Football team. Doug because he's such a jerk, and then Sam. For tallness."

"He thinks that tall people are the only ones who could hang the pictures and bash the angel," Bett explained to Dan. "Because he doesn't believe people can stand on chairs."

"Hey, you know what, whoever did it must have had goggles," said Dan. "To protect their eyes from all that glass from the cherub smashing. Idiot, you should have focused on the swim team. They come with goggles."

"Not so *loud*," Bett hissed, putting her arm around Ranger's skinny shoulders.

Dan turned to Bett. "Now we *have* to go to Anna's Art League or whatever thing. Just to see what people are talking about, if anyone suspects Mountain Lion Justice Boy here or has any other ideas."

Did he mean go together? Bett looked down and cleared her throat. "Do you know where and when it is? Did you already talk to Anna about it?"

"Yeah," said Dan. "It's going to be in one of the basement holes. Coyote Acres. Same stretch where Eddie threw Mutt's phone. Tonight at seven. I'll pick you up."

He'll pick me up.

Stop!

Ranger bounced on his toes. "I want to come! You guys have to let me come!"

"The hell we do," said Dan. "You can't be trusted to draw a circle, much less shut your mouth when you're in front of, like, victims of the crimes. We have to see how much of a mess you're in and figure out what's really going on."

"No fair!" cried Ranger, bouncing harder. "You all are an Art League and my posse's a Justice League! We could join forcescakes."

"Yeah, that's exactly what you should be thinking about, jagweed," said Dan, and led his brother back into the building. "You're the one who's going to burn if the other kids find out you drew those devils."

"Tufty-eared—"

"Shut up!"

Bett trailed behind, her mind off Ranger, suddenly shifting instead to tonight's meeting. She wondered if it was going to be a gathering of Twinklers, with her and Dan as the token Stays. Better to think about that than about being in a car alone with Dan.

39

TWO YEARS AGO . . . Bett pressed play.

"I have something to tell you all," the girl was saying. "I'm changing things up. No more cosmetics. I want to show you what I've found."

And the camera panned toward the bed, upon which lay a doll. Her clothes were beautiful—an angel robe with a halo. But the doll itself was creepy as hell. No eyes in its sockets. Just staring, empty holes.

Bett shuddered.

No. I can't. Press stop.

No way, bitch. This is what you get.

And Bett forced herself to look at the doll until anxiety and terror grew, until she had to go out of her bedroom window to one of her outside stashes and eat.

PART THREE

40

Thursday, Day Six of Grade Eleven, Late Afternoon

"WE'RE GOING TO AUNT JEANETTE'S FOR DINNER," Bett's mom told her when Eddie's bus had brought Bett home after detention. All had been quiet on that bus. Ranger and Mutt were tired out from practice, and besides, Bett and Dan had threatened Ranger within an inch of his life if he opened his mouth.

"What's going on?" Eddie had asked, looking at Bett and Dan in the mirror, his brows furrowed. "Are you two that mad you got detention?"

"No," Bett had said.

"We were just thinking about our wrongdoings," Dan improvised.

Mutt grunted. "Aren't you angels."

"Shut up, dillhole," said Dan.

And now here was Bett's mother, with folded arms and that look she got on her face when Bett was in trouble. "The school office called to let me know you had detention today. We will discuss why, in detail, at Aunt Jeanette's," she said.

"I can't come," said Bett. "I have to go out. A meeting. For school."

"Really," said Bett's mother. Her hair was particularly curly and pyramiddy today, what with the rain earlier. "You think you get detention and then you can just go out, la-di-da?"

"No," said Bett. "But it's for *school*. And all I got detention for was texting on the bus, and I was only texting because me and Dan didn't want to hurt his little brother's feelings."

"What brought on this noble sentiment?" asked her mother.

"He . . ." Bett thought quickly. "Ranger was wearing a stupid hat, and we were trying to think of ways to talk him out of it so he wouldn't get teased."

Bett's mother held out her hand for Bett's phone. Bett forked it over and prayed.

"All right," her mom said at last, after reading the texts. "But don't break rules like that in the future. Even to help a little kid. And why would he be scared about a hat when you have so much else going on over there? Seriously, Bett. I talked to your principal again today. Devil drawings?

Smashed glass? Why do I discuss everything with McLean before my own daughter?"

"I just got home!" Bett protested. "You know more than I do, up at the school with all your questioning. You're the one who doesn't tell *me* anything."

Bett's mother raised one eyebrow at her. "Be home by ten," she said finally. Bett's shoulders relaxed. "And quit texting when you aren't supposed to," she added, "or that phone becomes mine."

41

Autumn, Thursday,
Day Six of Grade Eleven, Evening

BETT WAS WAITING AT THE BOTTOM OF THE SLOPE FOR
Dan by ten of seven. She didn't want him to see the crazy
house shack she lived in now. It was weird enough, feeling
weird about Dan.

But all the weirdness left as soon as he pulled up in his
mother's station wagon. Bett half expected to see Ranger's
happy face popping up from the back seat.

"Hi," she said awkwardly.

"Hi," said Dan. Then: "Why don't you get in the car?"

"Oh, right." Bett got in the car and slammed the door.
She knew this wasn't a date or anything, but what if Dan
thought *she* thought it was? *Oh, crap. God, help me.*

"How's Ranger doing?" she asked Dan as he pulled
away along the dirt road.

"Able to keep his mouth shut so far," said Dan, driving with easy competence. "I guess that's something for someone whose ass is, like, way on the line."

"It is," said Bett. "I was worried he wasn't going to be able to take the pressure, and he'd start confessing all over the place."

"At least now we'll see if any of the kids at the meeting suspect anything about the little idiot," said Dan. "Then maybe we can intercede."

Bett nodded. Then, realizing he couldn't see her face in the dark, she said, "Yeah," instead. Intercede? But how?

By the time Dan and Bett reached the designated basement hole—the same one Mutt's phone had been thrown into, ironically—everybody else was already there. Someone had thoughtfully brought a rope ladder for people to climb down, and there was a tarp spread out over the dirt, which was still wet from the morning's rain, as well as a fire built in one of the basement corners. Bett was glad it was still humid out. She had taken another shower after she'd eaten and then let her hair dry naturally, so now it hung down her back in curls and waves. She'd used the flat iron on her bangs again, though, and she hoped they wouldn't frizz. She'd put product on them, but still.

Oh no! Would people think she was trying too hard? *Was* she trying too hard? She was! Why was she trying too hard? Was that a Plus?

Hester interrupted her thoughts.

"You really like those shorts, don't you, Bett?" she said as Bett climbed down the rope ladder, hideously aware that her butt was preceding her, jiggling as she climbed.

"You're a fine one to talk, Hester," said Anna as Bett jumped to the ground and looked at her, surprised. "How many times have we seen you in that embroidered cardigan?"

"I embroidered it myself," Hester protested.

"Well, I make my shorts myself," said Bett now, surprising herself.

"All right, then. So!" Now Anna addressed the clump of fifteen or twenty kids gathered in the center of the hole. *Ugh.* Bett had been right. Twinklers as far as the eye could see. "We're here to plan counter–Art Attacks."

"Oh," said Paul, his green seersucker suit dirtied by the climb down but not a hair out of place. "I just got that that's supposed to be like 'Heart Attacks.'"

"Yes," said Anna, staring at him. "That's what I was going for. Duh."

Bett looked across the basement hole and saw Mutt. Huh. She wouldn't have thought that an Art League or Art Attack or whatever this was would be his thing. But there he was, with a small girl by the hand, blond and tall for her age, with, as Bett's mother would have noted, wide-set eyes like Mutt. Well, at least that made two more Stays.

Something about that little girl was slightly familiar.

But what? Bett didn't know. She seemed sweet enough, carrying a stuffed animal in one hand and something else Bett couldn't make out in the other.

"I had to bring her," Mutt explained roughly, noticing Bett looking. "Babysitting."

"No problem," said Anna. "Can't hurt for kids to see how counteraction works. You're Meredith, right? What's your stuffy, sweetie?" she asked Mutt's sister.

The girl nodded. "A dog," she said softly, then half buried her face in Mutt's stomach. "Only his ears got torn off. My—"

Mutt pressed her shoulder and she stopped. Then she continued: "I like art, too. This is the goblet I made for school. It's going to be a present for my dad." She glanced up into Mutt's face as she spoke, but this time he didn't stop her talking. Bett wondered if Meredith's was the same goblet she had admired in art class just before Doug found that devil-tufty-mountain-lion drawing in his pocket.

"We should start this meeting," Paul said, and Anna nodded and turned back toward the group.

"So! We all know we have something seriously sick going on in our school," Anna began. "And we can't just keep letting it happen, even if we don't know who the asshole is."

Then they don't know Ranger is the devil-drawer. Yet. Bett breathed a sigh of relief and exchanged glances with Dan, but Dan still looked tense.

"And we think the way to fight destruction is with creativity—" Paul was continuing.

"So we have an idea," Anna broke in. "A two-part one."

"First, we want to do a graffiti mural," said Paul. "Not assholic graffiti like the destroyer did, but one about positive things."

"Then we'll sneak into the school at night and hang it up so people can see something *good* when they walk into the school!" Anna practically sang out.

"Why sneak in?" asked Mutt. "Why not just hang it at lunch?"

Paul held up a hand. "Because a) Anna has gotten detention twice for 'using evidence' to make new projects to replace the art that was destroyed," he said, "and b) kids need to be cheered up when they come into the school first thing. If *we're* freaked by all this, imagine what the elementary kids are hearing over on their side of the building—the kindergartners, for God's sake!"

It was true. Already parents of some of the younger kids were driving them to school or keeping them home.

Dan was nodding. Then he paused. "But what if we're, like, watched? By security cameras or something?"

"Here? In Salt River?" Paul exhaled. "If there were security cameras or alarms, the asshole would have been caught already," he said.

True enough.

"But I'll tell you what," Paul continued. "I sure as hell already feel watched—by whoever's doing this BS."

"Me too," said Anna. "Okay. Who's in?"

"Me!"

"Me!"

Everyone, apparently, wanted to work on the mural. Paul and Anna helped Hester and Lily spread out a gigantic piece of canvas on top of the tarp, other kids weighting down the curled corners with stones. Others set out markers and tempera paint pots with brushes, pencils and charcoal and all kinds of art supplies they'd brought with them. And soon hands were flying everywhere, all over that canvas, spray-painting and paint-painting and fast-drawing with markers and pens.

The mural began to take shape. In the middle of the canvas, Anna quickly sketched out the cherub. Paul and half a dozen others dove in along the sides, re-creating the pictures of the people who had been drawn with such care on the walls from the summer program, some in a cartoonish style and some mimicking the style in which they'd originally been drawn. Eli and the rest were spray-painting big, blocky, 3-D easy-looking letters saying ART ATTACK and CREATION and CREATIVITY WINS.

Bett stood back. Even though she believed in it, it was a tiny bit much for her. Pairs of worlds were colliding all over the place. School world with guys-at-lunch world, and bigger school world with Twinklers and Stays. Girls and normal people. The mix was not comfortable.

But the mixing of groups brought a torrent of thoughts rushing into Bett's mind, and she shook her head, hard, to rid herself of them. *No,* she told herself in the din of the noise from the group. *Don't think about her now. Stop.*

But Bett's left ear went out and the STOP was already worn off her sneaker sole and she couldn't not.

42

TWO YEARS AGO . . . "Why do you write words on your sneaker soles?" Stephanie had asked once. Bett hadn't thought Stephanie would notice. Or anyone.

She shrugged.

"What?" Stephanie persisted. "Aren't I your bestie? Can't you tell even me?"

Bett shrugged again. "It's dumb," she said. "And aren't we late to Paul's house?" Paul's family was having a party, and she and Stephanie had just spent forty-five minutes getting ready.

"Paul can wait," said Stephanie. "Tell me about your sneakers."

"I just write words on them," said Bett.

"Let me see," said Stephanie, and before Bett knew it, Stephanie had grabbed her foot and held it up to look at the sole.

"'**Toughness**,'" Stephanie read. "What does that even mean?" But she wasn't being snotty. Stephanie never was, only curious.

"It means . . . being tough. Like, when it's hard to run, and I'm exhausted and want to stop, it makes me keep going."

"So, like, you put traits on your shoe soles?"

"I guess," Bett admitted, feeling naked and dumb. "Yeah."

"That is so cool," said Stephanie warmly. "Bett, you are like Wonder Woman."

Bett said nothing, but she smiled and looked down.

If she wrote things on her sneaker soles, when the words had finally worn away, that should be it. The trait should be in her. It worked, you know. It really did.

43

Thursday, Sixth Day of Eleventh Grade, Nighttime at this Weird Art Meeting

"THIS IS ALL WELL AND GOOD, BUT WE HAVE TO MAKE another plan now." Dan stood over by the finished but still-wet mural. "To find out who did it all in the first place and turn them in."

"But what if that person turns out to be seriously mental? What if they come after us before we get them?" asked Eli. "Oh man, I want some wine. Or a beer." He laid his head on Paul's shoulder.

Paul put his arm around him, even as he whispered furiously, "Ixnay on the ineway and the eerbay," swinging his eyes over to Mutt's little sister.

"You guys drink?" Meredith's eyes were wide.

"No," chorused everybody, while Hester moved strategically in front of a cooler.

"I just meant 'whine,' like I want to 'whine' about the situation," Eli told Meredith.

"I was told this meeting would be part party," another boy interrupted.

"You were told wrong," said Anna with another eyeswing at Meredith.

Dan sighed. "Let's get back to business."

But before she could help herself, Bett blurted out, "I think I have a clue." The heat of the fire baked her right side. "There was dirt around the transom this morning," she said. "It went all the way to the window in the second-floor front stairwell."

"So what?" asked Hester.

"You don't get it—" Bett began.

"*Oh,*" said Dan. "You mean you think that the person must have broken into the school at night, like we're planning to, and they went in through that second-floor window. Smashed the cherub thing, then left the same way."

"Exactly," said Bett, relieved.

"But how would the perp get up there?" asked Hester.

"Perpcakes," muttered Bett without thinking. Then: "Kind of easy," she said, louder. "Just swing up over the porch roof thing above the front entrance and then open the window and you're in. If the perp—"

"—if the perp unlocked the window in the day, then they could get in at night, easycakes." Anna finished Bett's sentence and grinned at her. Was she making fun of her?

"By the way, I think we need just a *few* people to break in to hang this mural," said Dan. "Not too many of us or it's too risky. We have to bust in quietly, hang our mural, and then get the hell out of there."

"But if we bust in, won't we make a whole lot of noise?" asked Eli.

"*YES!*" said Dan. "That's why I keep saying just a few of us and not the whole group! Like, five kids. We need the strongest and quickest of us who can also keep their mouths shut."

"Like . . . ?" Paul prompted.

"You," said Dan. "For one. But our leader, I think, should be Bett."

Every head swiveled toward Bett. It was awful. "No," she said.

"Yes," Dan insisted. "You're fast. You're strong. And you love this shit."

"I do not love this shit," Bett argued. But already her heart was racing because she did love this shit. "Besides, it would be stupid to try your luck climbing up to the front window again," she added. "If I saw that dirt, so did an adult."

"I don't know about that," said Eli. "We have some pretty out-of-it teachers in our school."

Bett nodded. True that. "Well, anyway, I bet the first-floor windows will be locked so you'll need one person to scale up the wall to the back second-floor window," said Bett. "The window in the middle. And then that person needs to let everybody else in through the side gym door after they get in."

"Sounds like a plan," said Anna.

"Who do you all think the psycho is?" asked Hester abruptly.

"My money's on Doug," said Paul, even though Mutt was right there and Doug was one of Mutt's main meat minions. "He's such a dick. I can see him doing shit like this without even thinking. And planting a picture on himself, thinking he's throwing off suspicion. That's a real television crime drama move right there."

"And also, remember that time he chainsawed the furniture when Kelley had that party when her parents were out of town? He *is* a psycho," claimed Eli.

They all remembered that time. Kelley had been grounded for months.

"It's not Doug," said Mutt unexpectedly. "You may think he's a dick, but he's not the kind of dick who plans."

Nobody had a response to that.

Meredith looked scared.

"Don't worry," Mutt told her. "And don't you tell anyone about any of this, either."

"I won't," Meredith promised, clutching her goblet and earless dog.

"The question now is, who's going to scale the school?"

Paul asked. "That's going to be tricky. No porch on the back side to get a boost from."

There was a silence. Then: "Bett," said Dan. "You remember that video? Bett on the bike?"

Hester clicked her tongue.

They remember the video? Bett thought wildly.

"I loved that video," Anna said.

"Shit, y'all, I still HAVE that video," said Eli, and he pulled out his phone. "I'll send Anna the link and we can all watch it on both phones."

"No!" protested Bett, but it was too late.

Bett on the bike, coasting off the rock and flying. Sliding into the water. Bill's hand pulling her up. Replay. Replay. Replay.

44

Thursday, Night of the Sixth
Eleventh Grade Day, Later, Basement Hole

"COME ON, BETT!"

"Do it!"

"Please! You're the only one who can!"

"NO!" Bett said, stepping back. Why had she even brought up the idea in the first place?

"But we need you," said Anna pleadingly. "Anyone who can do that can scale one stupid story of a stupid stone school."

"Lots of handholds in stone," Dan added.

"Then *you* do it," Bett snapped. "I can't do it. I can't." In no way was she going to do another Fizzicle Feet, especially not one as Plus as this one. She had vowed, and the vow made sense because she wasn't going to do one and enjoy it and then come down and nearly kill someone and get their eyes out of their head and—

"Please?" Dan said. "For me? And"—he lowered his voice—"for Ranger?"

Bett thought about Ranger with his eyes filled with tears because he was afraid he'd be hung for the psycho.

She was still.

The Art League waited.

"Okay," Bett said finally. "I'll do it. But I want Dan . . . Paul . . . Anna, and . . . one more with me."

"Jesus, not me, please," said Eli.

"No, honey," said Paul. "Not you. What about you, Mutt? You're strong."

"No," said Mutt and Bett simultaneously.

Mutt glared at her. "I have to be home for Meredith," he said.

"Who, then?" Paul asked.

"I'll go," said Hester. "I've done gymnastics since I was three. I've got good reflexes."

Oh, great, thought Bett. But "Fine" was all she said. "Now let's figure this out. We have to wait for this mural to dry and then we can make our move."

Paul nodded. "Tomorrow night we take back the school."

Bett made it home by ten, but only just. The phone was ringing, but the house was empty—her mother must still be at Aunt Jeanette's. Bett saw the number on the phone.

Her father. She picked the phone up and breathed into it.

"Bett?" asked her father. "Is that you?"

Bett didn't answer. "Honey, we can't keep going on like this. You have to forgive me at some point."

"For being a cheater?" asked Bett. "For not caring about anyone but yourself?"

"Bett, don't be rude."

"Don't you pretend you're an actual parent who can tell me what to do," said Bett, and hung up the phone.

Bett's mom finally came home an hour later. "How was your evening?" she asked Bett.

"Fine," said Bett, and was surprised that this was true. Her stomach began to churn.

"Great!" said her mother. "I'm glad, honey. Who else was at your meeting?"

"Oh, just Dan and Paul and that assholic Mutt and people. Mutt had to bring his little sister."

"Those poor kids." Her mom sighed. "They didn't exactly win the parent lottery. Thank God that little girl has Mutt to look out for her, even if he is, as you say, assholic." She paused. "Anyone else there?" she asked lightly.

Bett hesitated. "Anna Reed. Hester O'Reilly. Some other Twinklers."

Her mother was trying not to smile, and Bett knew it wasn't about her Twinkler comment, but because Bett had been with girls as well as boys—hell, with people, period.

Stop staring at me.

She turned and went up the four stairs to her room and, twisting her hair into its topknot, got into bed, covers over her head, clothes still on. She knew she'd be making a midnight snack run. Her heart was pounding.

45

Thursday, Extra Late,
So Late It's Friday, Really

BETT'S CHEST ROILED AND THE FAMILIAR ANXIETY built and built until, around one, when she knew her mother was finally asleep, she climbed out of her bedroom window and landed on the damp, soft dirt below. It was so easy to escape her room in this tiny house. Her mother hadn't factored that into her planning when she'd built it, Bett bet. She had just been so glad to get out of the old house. As, of course, had Bett, even if she couldn't let herself think about that too hard.

Bett picked her way to the river slope where she'd found a little rock cave, no bigger than a bread box, the entrance of which she'd covered with a stone. She shoved that rock aside now and there, in her hiding place, were the four cupcakes she'd bought last weekend from the supermarket. She sat beside the little cavern, river rushing, night all over, dark like a cloak and the deep smell of water and the woods and her cupcakes.

Everything was too much. One by one, she ate all four of the cupcakes, breaking them in half across the cake part and putting the bottom half over the frosting to make cup-cake sandwiches out of them.

She should go back to the house. But she didn't want to. What had she gotten herself into with this cross-country team and now Ranger and this Fizzicle Feet and people like Dan kept talking to her and Dan's hair was the good kind of red?

Across the oxbow—an almost circular bend of the river—a house stood, one light on like a beacon under an old, old tree. *Then the waders man is a neighbor,* thought Bett, and wondered why he'd built his house on an oxbow. But maybe the oxbow was new. There had been that big hurricane four years ago or so; maybe the river had over-flowed and pinched off the man's land. Maybe he felt he had a choice—either live in his house or abandon it—and he picked the oxbow. At least there was a small bridge of land still connecting the O of his property to the mainland.

Despite herself, Bett approved of his choice. *It must feel good,* she thought. *Walking through the river like that and fishing.* She thought about the man again.

From high up on Bett's slope, the fields beyond the river and oxbow were visible in the pale moonlight, and she realized that I Know a Guy Field was right behind the oxbow. Waders Man must own it!

Should she ask Eddie about him? See if the man was still a therapist?

Oh, why did she care if he was?

But she did.

She waited, watching the man's house. Finally, his light went out, so Bett made her way back up to her window and bed.

46

Friday,
the Seventh Day of Eleventh Grade

THE NEXT AFTERNOON, ANNA STOOD AT THE DOOR OF their bus after school. What was that about?

Eddie wondered, too. "Who are you? And to what do I owe this pleasure?"

"I'm Anna Reed," said Anna. "And I want to join the cross-country team."

What? Why was Anna joining the team? The answer came to Bett in a very few minutes, when Dan approached the bus and stood behind Anna.

Of course, Bett thought. *Anna likes Dan.*

Her heart sank. And the sinking took her off guard. *Shut up*, she told it. *Anna is pretty and thin and creative and why wouldn't he like her back?*

"You want to join," said Eddie to Anna. "Well, it's not

as easy as that. There are forms to fill out. And I don't even know if you can run."

"I have the forms," said Anna, waving them. "I got them from Mrs. Schlovsky. And even if I suck at running, everyone else is good. Can't I at least try?"

Eddie held out his hand for the forms. "They seem to be in order," he said, flicking through them. "All right. Get the hell on my bus."

Anna got the hell on his bus. She scooted into the seat in front of Bett. Her head came up over the seat as she turned and knelt to face Bett.

"Is this in any way fun?" she whispered.

"No," Bett whispered back.

"SIT DOWN!" shouted Eddie from his driver's seat.

Anna turned around and sat down.

"You get used to the yelling," Ranger told her friendlily.

Once on the field, Eddie was in a mood. He kept the bus stereo on, blasting "Hotel California" while they stretched, and then, after that, "More Than a Feeling," which at least didn't make Bett want to put a fork in her eye, but was still such a seventies Mom song that she felt like she was in forced time travel yet again. Why did she have to be stuck in Salt River with nothing and nobody and all these adults fastened to the past?

"All right," said Eddie, when the stretching was done. "Twice around the field and then the long course again. Two circles around."

JUST WRECK IT ALL

"Can't we at least shake it up a little?" asked Dan. "Can we, like, go left first today after the warm-up laps?"

Eddie considered. "Fine," he said. "I guess I see no harm in that." He turned to Bett and then toward Anna. "You two run the warm-up together. Two laps around the field and no cutting corners."

Anna looked nervous. Bett looked at her and shrugged. "Just do a walk-jog," she said. "You'll make it."

And they began. Anna really was slow, Bett realized. Or maybe she was just conserving her energy for the long course ahead of them. She was puffing pretty hard already, though. Perhaps Bett had made a mistake choosing Anna for the elite force after all.

But Bett only pointed toward the gap in the fence and said, "That's where we run out to the road. When we've done the two warm-up laps."

Anna nodded, her face already flushed.

Chug chug chug. HONK!

"Get up GET UP *GET UP!*" Eddie was yelling out the bus window behind them. "You call that a warm-up? You're almost walking!"

Anna gaped at Bett, clearly terrified.

"He just chases us," Bett told her, realizing that was no comfort. And chase them he did, shouting, zigging around the field so they had to avoid his bus until they were finally on the road and he could chase them for real.

"GET UP, BETT!"

"WATCH THE ROAD!" Bett screamed back. Surely,

this counted as distracted driving. But no. While Eddie let Anna slip back to jog-walk behind the bus, he was pursuing Bett in his single-minded way. He picked up speed. So did Bett.

The crazy bastard was going to hit her.

But he didn't. He got her around the course, and soon she was passing Ranger and then Dan and was up with Mutt, five yards between them in the end.

"THAT," said Eddie, once practice was over and they were all back on the bus, "is what I'm talking about. That is what I want to see in the meet, Bett, and I won't be able to chase you with a bus then."

"Meet?"

"What meet?"

"I *told* you fools," said Eddie. "We got a late start to the season, but the first meet is tomorrow."

"I forgot!"

"I don't care! Be at school by six a.m. We got to get there early so we can walk the course first."

Six a.m.! Dan exchanged glances with Bett. Tonight was Break-In Night. How could they possibly be awake enough to run a 5K the next morning?

"Let's hope for adrenaline," said Dan, clearly reading her mind, as the bus pulled up to the school. He and Anna got off the bus together and walked toward the gym door and the locker rooms.

"Eddie?" Bett stood in the entry to the bus. "Who's 'I

Know a Guy'? The one who owns the field? What's his name?"

"Why do you ask?" asked Eddie, his voice wary. "I like to keep my real life separate from you twerps."

"He's our new neighbor, is all, and I forget his name," Bett said. "I just wanted to thank him for letting us use the field next time I see him."

"Oh," said Eddie. "Well. In that case. It's Hugh Munin."

"Yes!" said Bett as soon as he said it. She remembered now. Hugh Munin. She wanted to ask if Mr. Munin was still a therapist at the vet center, but she certainly wouldn't disrespect Eddie's business and bring that up now. What would it be like to have, like, a conversation with Hugh Munin now, away from the river? But she immediately quelled the thought. "Thank you," she said to Eddie, a little too loudly.

"Whatever." Eddie shrugged. Bett ran into the locker room, tightening her topknot on the way.

Friday Evening

BETT LEFT THE SIM CARD HOUSE AND WENT DOWN TO
the edge of the slope that led to the river. Not the cupcake
cave slope. The one where a person could walk into the
only part of the river where she might dare to swim, if it
were the hottest day of the year and she were willing to
put on a bathing suit, none of which in existence would
fit Bett. But it was the best view of Hugh Munin's house,
and Bett wanted to get an eyeful. Call it a compulsion. Or
a mortification.

He was there, in the river, fishing rod in hand.

Relief washed over Bett. "Mr. Munin!" she called to him.

The man turned around, surprised. "You remember my
name?" he shouted to her.

Bett nodded.

The man turned and walked toward her. Bett jumped.

"I'm sorry." Mr. Munin stopped. "I didn't mean to scare you."

Should she go?

Mr. Munin turned as if to walk back across the river to his house, fishing rod in hand like a bow.

"How do you know Eddie?" Bett blurted, and Mr. Munin turned again to face her.

But he didn't answer her question. Instead, he said, "Eddie told me if I saw you to tell you he's so glad to work with you."

Bett started. "You know he's my coach?"

"Yes. I've known Eddie for years. We like to chat."

"Why did you stay in your house even after the river made the oxbow?" Why was she asking that? She wanted to know about Eddie—but her mouth was behaving independently from her mind. Or maybe reflecting it, because Bett didn't know what she wanted.

"I love my home," he said simply.

Bett hesitated. "It must feel good," she said. "Walking through the river like that."

"It does to me," said Mr. Munin. "I love fishing, and I don't mind getting a little wet. I have a good woodstove."

He hesitated, his dark eyes looking into Bett's. "Eddie really cares about you."

Bett snorted. "Is that why he chases me with a bus?"

"Yes," said Mr. Munin, smiling. Then the smile faded.

"He also said to tell you he just wants to talk to you."

Bett was silent.

"It's not going to be scary," said Mr. Munin.

"Yes, it is, actually." And Bett turned away from him quickly and hurried back to her house and scaled the wall into her own little room, bypassing the door and the possibility of her mother. Outside her window she could see Hugh Munin standing there in the water, ready to make the crossing to his house.

48

Friday Night/Saturday Morning,
Autumn Still

THE FIVE OF THEM—ANNA, DAN, HESTER, PAUL, AND
Bett—huddled in the hedges at the back of the school. The
hedges were large enough that all five kids could squat in
there and not be seen from the road, thank God. They had
all managed to escape their houses to meet here at one a.m.
Bett was the only one who had done it by window, though.
And now here she was, at the bottom of the back wall of
the school with these four yahoos, supposed to be ready to
climb the wall.

"I'm already wiped out from that practice," said Anna
softly. "I didn't know it would be so awful."

"Poor baby," murmured Paul comfortingly.

"At least you didn't have the bus chase you the whole
way," whispered Dan. "Bett, I don't know how you put up
with that."

"I put up with it or get creamed," whispered Bett back. "You all, can we talk a minute? About this perp? Because my mom always says it's good to know the psychology of your criminal before you head into their turf. And our school counts as their turf, I think."

"Yeah," said Dan. "In this instance, I think you're right."

"We know it's someone angry," said Anna.

No shit, thought Bett, but she was nice out loud. "Right."

"And it has to be someone who hates our school," added Dan.

"Isn't that all of us?" asked Paul.

"I mean, *hate*-hate," said Dan. "And someone strong enough to, like, wield a hatchet over a transom."

"And tall enough!"

It was Ranger, popping out of the hedges like an oversize and unwelcome robin.

"What the hell are you doing here?" whisper-screamed Dan.

"Helping," said Ranger brightly. "It's no fair of you guys to leave me out. I heard you on your phone, Dan. I knew something was up! I'm little but I'm quick—I'm almost as fast as you are." This was true. "And I want to help."

"Jesus Christ!" said Paul.

"Ranger," said Bett. "This is really important, and really risky. You are already practically in trouble for real."

"Why?" asked Paul.

"For sneaking out," said Dan hastily, exchanging

anguished glances with Bett. "Dude, this could put you over the edge if you get caught."

Bett hoped Ranger caught the double meaning.

Anna glanced at them both. "Well, he's already here. We're sort of stuck with him."

Dan looked at her in disbelief.

Anna shrugged. "What are you going to do, bring him home now? Maybe he can stay here and be the lookout or something."

"I'm not being any lookout!" Ranger cried.

"Shut up," the rest of them hissed at once.

"This is exactly what we mean," said Dan. "You are too stupid to be quiet even when it's your own head on the chopping block."

Ranger's face grew serious in an instant. "I will shut up," he whispered. "I promise. Cakes."

"So that's where you got that from!" Anna beamed at Bett, then at Ranger. Bett felt a pang—Ranger was *her* little tadpole.

"Can we get back to the plan?" asked Paul. "Or will there be more seventh-grade idiots who show up to 'help' us?" His fingers twitched with the air quotes.

"It's just me," Ranger promised. "I didn't even tell Martin and Joaquin."

"How'd you get here, by the way?" asked Dan.

"Back of the car," said Ranger. "I've been hiding there since after dinner."

"What?!" Dan squawked.

"Impressive," said Hester.

"Anyway," said Paul. "Back to business. So we know the person is angry."

"And has spray paint."

"And a hatchet."

"Or access to one."

Bett went still.

A hatchet. The fire hatchet by the first aid kit on the bus. That hatchet could have been used to slash the pictures and the wings *and* smash the angel the kid vet had made. And anybody could buy a can of spray paint. In addition to his kidnapping them as an introduction to the cross-country team and general weirdness and messed-upness from war.

Oh my God, the psycho might be Eddie.

Bett's heart pounded. She had to talk to Dan. Alone. But they *weren't* alone.

But it made sense. Eddie hated war. He sought psychological services. That cherub made by the kid who died from a war—that kind of thing could have put him over the edge. Eddie could've come into the school on the first day no problem and slashed those pictures, too. He wouldn't have even had to sign in at the office, because he was an employee. And Ranger's break-in theory made sense for the angel smashing and wing slashing. Though Eddie was kind of hefty to imagine him slinging himself over the rain roof above the school entrance.

Well, I'm hefty, too, Bett thought. And she could certainly climb up on that damn porch thing if she wanted to,
without the benefit of military training.

"Are we ready?" Paul whispered.

"Ready," said the others.

"What's the warning if you see someone coming?"

"Three foot stomps," said Dan.

"Or a damn scream if you get separated," said Anna.

"No screaming," said Bett. "But, Ranger, you hoot like
an owl if you see something out here."

"I'm not staying out here," Ranger repeated stubbornly.

"Yes, you are!"

"No, I'm not!"

Several rounds of this and everyone gave in. What
else could they do? So it was six of them who stole quietly out of the hedges and approached the back of the
school.

Bett stared up at the wall everyone expected her to climb.
Sure, Paul had unlatched the window and loosened the
screen up there earlier in the day, but was she going to be
able to hang on to the ledge of the sill and push the window
open, too? She eyed potential footholds.

"We should have brought that rope ladder we had at
the meeting in the basement hole," said Paul, the mural
folded and stuffed under his hoodie. Everybody gave him
a look.

"Great timing for the safety thought, bro," said Dan.

Bett's left ear began to roar. She hadn't done anything like this in so long. "Nobody video me," she said, still surveying the wall. She could see several grips. *Good.* "I mean it." That was all she needed, a video of her fat ass heading up the wall.

"We promise," said Anna earnestly. "We don't want photographic evidence, anyway. We're technically doing a B and E, even if it is for good."

Bett looked at Anna with respect. How did she know the term "B and E"?

"I watch a lot of cop shows," Anna said, another mind reader.

Bett turned back to the stone wall. *Okay,* she told herself. *This is to keep Ranger safe. And to see what the hell is up with Eddie.* Already she could feel the adrenaline starting.

Don't think of it like a Fizzicle Feet, she told herself firmly. *Don't or you'll die. Think of it as helping. It's the only way.*

And she stood back, swung her arms, and jumped, catching two stone handholds straight off the bat.

"Badass!" whispered Paul below.

Bett used her feet to work her way up, and then found two more pieces of rough rock to grasp.

This is easy, she thought, and was surprised to find herself disappointed.

Below her, the worried faces of the mixed Art and

Justice and Cross-Country Leagues, Twinklers and Stays, looked up at her.

But Bett couldn't think about anything but the climb now. And with just two more swings and grabs, Bett was at the window.

"Go," she whispered to the others once she'd balanced herself on the sill ledge, pushed up the window with one hand, and heaved herself into the school. "Go to the gym door. Now!"

"Wait," whispered Hester fiercely. "I'm going up there, too. Give me a boost, you guys. Bett, you can catch my hands and pull me up."

"No," said Bett.

"Yes!" said Hester. "It's not fair if you're the only one caught. Plus, I can help keep an eye out from the inside."

Hester was willing to put herself on the line with her? Huh!

"Okay." Bett gave in. "Boost her, you all."

So the other four hoisted Hester up and Bett caught her hands and seconds later Hester was over the sill with Bett.

"MOVE!" Bett whisper-shouted down to the others. As they dashed off, Bett pulled the screen down and locked the window again. She and Hester had landed in the English room. In front of them was a table full of new copies of a book—*The Prose and Poetic Eddas*—that Bett guessed was next on the docket after Virginia Woolf.

"What the hell is a prose and poetic edda?" whispered Hester.

"No idea," Bett answered. "Come on. Let's go. We have to let the others in."

Bett quickly checked her sneakers for dirt, but they seemed clean enough, despite her having been chased by a bus in them for the past several days.

Better get a move on.

Hester and Bett stole their way downstairs, hugging the walls until they reached the gym door. Even though they opened it as slowly and carefully as they could, the door let out an enormous creak and Bett almost had a heart attack.

She wasn't alone. "I almost had a heart attack," whispered Dan, slipping into the gym.

"Me too!" Hester added.

"An Art Attack heart attack," Ranger began until they all glared him quiet.

They crept through the first floor. Not a soul. The swimming pool was quiet. The library and most all of the classroom doors were closed. They checked carefully behind each one, but there was nothing. And no one.

"Let's make sure the upstairs is clear," Bett suggested, but she pulled on Dan's arm to hold him back as the others headed up.

"Dan," she whispered when they were out of earshot. "I think Eddie may be the perp."

"Are you crazy?" Dan whispered back, looking around

nervously. "He's weird, yeah, but he's not mental."

"He is a little bit, I think. And he has the means." Bett explained about the hatchet.

Dan hesitated. "But why? You were just going on about the psychology five minutes ago. Eddie doesn't hate the school. So what gives?"

"Well, he *is* angry as hell all the time," said Bett. "He's always about to pop."

Dan's brow furrowed. "That's true."

"And I know he has, like, trauma from that war."

Dan frowned. "But the angel was made by a vet. Wouldn't Eddie want to preserve that, not smash it?"

"Maybe," said Bett. "Or maybe war just triggers him and he couldn't stand it, walking through the school. Or maybe he's just anti-angel."

"And anti–kid art? It makes him want to 'gut this place'? Come on."

"No, *you* come on. If it *is* Eddie, we have to get him help." Bett's mind was racing again. Could she get him to Hugh Munin so he could help in his sure, dependable way, and then maybe Eddie would be okay? Eddie was a nut, but she didn't want him in jail, for God's sake.

"Bett! Dan! Get up here!" Hester whisper-called from above.

They took the stairs two at a time and joined the others on the second-floor landing.

CLANG!

Bett jumped. What the hell was that?

CLANG!

They all looked at each other in alarm.

Was it coming from the outside?

CLANG!

Bett ran toward the window, toward the sound, Hester and Dan right behind her. The others were frozen in place.

CLANG!

Then Bett froze, too, staring out at the entrance to the school.

CLANG!

Staring.

Because someone was by the statue of the soldier on the stone steps of the school, someone with a hatchet, someone bashing the shit out of the man in his coat.

But it wasn't Eddie.

CLANG!

It was Mutt.

Saturday Morning, Autumn,
Wee but Terrifying Hours

"WHAT?!" GASPED PAUL. BETT THREW OPEN THE window and now they all hung out, horrified, as Mutt— Mutt!!—smashed at the statue of the man. But the bronze must have been tough and the hatchet not enough because they could hear Mutt grunting and weeping with frustration.

Bett was in disbelief. Mutt?! MUTT? But—but—he had been as pissed off as anyone about what was happening! And wasn't he the one who'd gone on and on about other people destroying stuff that first day at lunch?

"Come on," said Bett. "We have to stop him."

Anna held back. "He has a hatchet," she said, her voice trembling.

"I don't think it's us he's after," Dan said, and so the six of them pounded down the stairs and flung open the door, and there was Mutt, hatchet midswing.

"What the hell?!" shouted Paul. "What the eff are you doing?"

Mutt froze, startled. Then he looked terrified.

"Mutt, stop! What is wrong with you?!" cried Bett.

Bett was furious, incredulous, petrified all at once.

But then she saw.

Mutt's face. One eye black and swollen near shut. The other flowing with tears of rage.

"Shut up!" Mutt cried, turning away from them with another swing of the hatchet. "Shut up, you assholes with your perfect lives." *CLANG!* "ART ATTACK! Angel heads! Peace and love and all that crap. You don't know anything!"

Bett's thoughts skittered crazily. She certainly wasn't going to get near Mutt and that hatchet, but she knew she had to get him to drop it.

"Mutt," she said, forcing her voice to be low and steady. *Have to stay calm.* "Put the hatchet down, put it down, and no one will know it's you except us. Just stop now and we'll keep it a secret."

Behind her, Ranger was gulping.

"I will not stop now!" Mutt's voice was nearly a shriek. "Dog one night, cup the next! Police at the house every five seconds and that damned social worker, too! What the hell is the point?"

What was he talking about?

Then Bett's breath caught. That call that had come across her mother's radio. Mutt's eye. Oh, his eye, so swollen. His own knuckles bloodied.

Anna came closer. "Mutt," she began, but she was cut off by the piercing sound of a siren, a siren loud and familiar to Bett, and her stomach dropped. She knew exactly who that siren belonged to, who was coming their way.

Yep.

Soon the flashing blue lights of a cop van were swirling over their faces as Bett's mother got out of the vehicle. She laser-beamed on Mutt immediately.

"Mutt Igdris! What the hell is wrong with you?" Bett's mother demanded.

Mutt dropped the hatchet. Immediately.

Bett's mom carefully picked it up and put it in a plastic bag while Mutt stood panting beside her.

"I'm taking you in. All of you," she said, her eyes sweeping the group. Then they landed on Bett, went wide, then *furious*. "WHAT THE HELL IS THE MATTER WITH YOU?" she screamed. "Sneaking out? *Vandalism*? Damaging *town property*?"

"I didn't damage anything!" Bett cried out. "None of us did! Only Mutt!"

"Only Mutt with you all as an audience egging him on," said a male voice, and there was Mr. McLean, coming out of the other side of the police van. Mr. McLean?

Oh my God, we're in hell.

"That's it," Bett's mother decided. "All of you. Into the van." And just like on TV, she read them their rights and cuffed Mutt.

"You can't arrest us!" cried Anna.

"I can," said Bett's mother wearily. "And before we get in that van, I want any and all arms surrendered."

"Any and all arms surrendered?" Paul's voice was puzzled.

Oh, God. Doesn't he get it?

But no. As if she were psychic, it happened just the way Bett thought it would with this group of yahoos. They shoved their arms forward, skin shining in the moonlight and fingers flashing blue in the light of the police car.

Ranger was still stuck behind the bigger kids, desperately trying to shove his way in. "Bett, do you think your mom'll arrest me because my arms don't reach?"

"You guys!" Bett cried, exasperated. "She means guns!"

But she stood beside Dan and stuck her arms out alongside the others' anyway.

50

Still Wee Hours of Saturday

IT WAS COMPLETE CHAOS. BETT, DAN, RANGER, Anna, Paul, Hester, and Mutt were brought down to the station house. Parents were called. Mutt with his blackened eye was still in handcuffs. The rest of them were lined up for questioning, sitting on hard chairs, not daring to move more than was necessary, but all of them ready to blow.

"We just wanted to put up some more art!" Paul said for the tenth time, his voice sounding closer and closer to cracking.

"Yeah?" said Bett's mom. "That's interesting because it seemed more like you were bashing it *down*." And she held out the hatchet in its plastic bag.

"That statue is *ruined*," said Mr. McLean. What was

he doing here, anyway? Did he get an automatic call for school-related matters? And how did they find out so quickly? Maybe the front door was wired after all. "Do you know what it means to our school? To our *community*?"

"Yes!" cried Dan.

"We do!" cried Anna.

"My *grandfather* is on that statue!" Paul yelped.

"So is my uncle!"

"Mutt, your own father is on the statue! You bragged about it yourself! What the fuck, man?" Dan was livid. "And what happened to your eye? Did you hit yourself with the hatchet while you were busy being a prick?"

"What were *any* of you thinking?" Bett's mother took a deep breath. "Help me understand. If you cared so much about your relatives, why would you destroy that statue?"

"It wasn't *us*!"

"Just Mutt!"

"Destruction of municipal property is a felony in this state. So is breaking and entering. . . . Look, we don't want to arrest you," said Bett's mom. "But you're making it hard for us not to."

Bett interrupted. "Please, Mom, just listen! We—not Mutt—the rest of us—we *did* break into the school. But not to destroy anything. Why would we break *in* if the statue was outside? We broke in to—"

"Combat the destruction at the school!" Anna finished

the sentence for her. Her fists were clenched. She looked around wildly. "Where is the mural? Paul had it—"

"You mean this?" And Bett's mother held up the folded piece of canvas, also in a plastic bag.

"Yes," said Paul. "Please! Let us show you. May we . . . Are we allowed to stand?"

Bett's mother nodded. "Slowly, though." And she handed Paul the bag.

Anna and Paul stood and unfurled the mural between them. Mr. McLean and Bett's mom took it in.

"We were going to hang it in the foyer!" Hester explained, her hand rubbing a scrape she'd gotten from her boost up the wall. "We're *innocent*!"

Mr. McLean's nostrils flared. "Not of breaking into the school, young lady. And something *was* wrecked," he persisted. "That statue is a huge part of our town history and now it's severely damaged. I hope not irreparably."

"It was only Mutt who did that part!" Ranger had been so stoic on the ride to the station, but now he burst into tears. "We were just being a Justice League!"

Bett's mother gave her head a shake. "A what?"

The room exploded in shouts.

"Mutt's the one who's been smashing shit!"

"He did the graffiti—"

"He wrecked the art—"

"And the angel—"

"Shut up!" Mutt begged, his head in his hands.

"You asshole! We trusted you!"

"And leaving those sick drawings in people's pockets!"

"I didn't do those!"

"The hell you didn't!"

In the burst of shouts and questions, parents were entering the police station and finding their various kids and either immediately launching into yelling at them or wrapping their arms around them, depending. It was complete pandemonium. In the midst of it all, Bett's mom grabbed her by the elbow and steered her into her office, face full of fury and confusion.

"Bett," she said, "what the hell is really going on?" The office was spare, but full of pictures of Bett: Bett younger on sports teams, Bett's school pictures, toddler Bett jumping off the back of a sofa, preschool Bett climbing trees as high as she could.

It was all too much.

"What?"

"Don't get smart with me!"

"I'm not!" cried Bett. "I can't hear you very well!"

Her mother's face softened immediately. "I'm so sorry, Bett. Oh, honey. Your ear. The siren." She spoke directly into Bett's face, so that Bett could see her lips. Bett turned her good, right ear toward her mother. "Can you talk to me?" her mother asked in a loud, clear voice.

And Bett told her. Everything. The slashing, the tufty-eared mountain lions of justice, Ranger's Justice League and the new Art League, the break-in, everything. Everything except her false suspicion of Eddie.

"So the kid who did the pictures is that little dude?"

"Yes," said Bett.

"And the pictures were supposed to be of what again?"

"Tufty-eared mountain lions of . . ."

Bett trailed off. Through the window of her mom's office, Bett saw the last parent came in. Longish blond hair, too tan. Wide-set eyes. Bruise on his jaw.

Bett recognized him at once.

Oh my God, why hadn't she seen it before? Mutt's dad was the guy from Fancy Jim's all that long time ago. Meredith, Mutt's little sister, was the perfect little girl who was there that day, the little girl Bett let drive home with an alcohol-stinking man.

Out in the main room Mutt's swollen face went dead and gray as his dad stood over him and boomed hell at him from above.

51

Saturday Morning, If the Hours Could Be Any Wee-er, This Is Them

BETT WAS SURE THE KIDS ON THE CROSS-COUNTRY TEAM were going to be banned from the meet the next day but, "Oh, no," her mother told her. "All of you on that team, except Mutt Igdris, will be waking up in two hours and getting on that bus and running that race."

"Fine," said Bett. "I'm dying to. You know how much I love cross-country."

Her mother made a face.

52

Saturday, Nearly Morning, Horribly

WHEN BETT CAME OUT OF HER MOM'S OFFICE, ONLY Mutt was left. His father was talking to the sergeant at the desk. Mutt moved up the row of chairs and sat next to Bett.

What the hell? Is he going to ask me to intervene with my mom?

But no.

"You look like shit," he said.

"You smell like it," said Bett back.

Mutt sucked his teeth. "I only meant you look tired."

Bett looked at the sergeant, then back at Mutt. "Why are you sitting with me?" she asked.

Mutt was quiet. "I don't know." He looked down at his handcuffs and let his hands fall, wrists red from the metal and from Mutt's own rubbing.

"Mutt," Bett asked gently, though she knew the answer already, "what happened to your eye?"

But Mutt was silent.

Ask an easier question.

"How did you get the hatchet?" she tried.

"I got a key to the bus," said Mutt, shrugging. "Perk of being the assistant coach."

Bett hesitated. "But why? Why would you wreck all that art? Why Anna's? Why did you wreck it all?"

Mutt shook his head and shrugged, and even though he looked away from her, Bett could see he was blinking back tears.

Bett shook her head. Why would Mutt have even come to the Art League meeting, then? But the answer came to her as quickly as the thought. Surveillance. Mutt wanted to know what the rest of them knew. He wanted to track what they were up to. Bett shivered. It was one thing to go to protect Ranger, and another to go to plan his next attack. But why would he bash the statue?

"Mutt," she said at last, "don't you know that now you're a *felon*?"

"I know," Mutt said at last. "You don't think I know? But—and this is the truth—those devil heads weren't me. And they're way more psycho, if you ask me."

Bett ignored that. She and her mother had agreed it would only complicate things to involve Ranger. Besides, the kid was so scared Bett was sure he'd never even so much as look at a crayon again, much less draw anything.

"Not more psycho than that graffiti you left. What did that even mean?"

Mutt looked at his hands again, full of little cuts from the hatchet. He paused. Then, so quietly Bett could hardly hear him: "You all just make me so mad."

Bett was silent, thinking, thinking. What had Mutt meant before by "the cup"? What cup? Oh! Mutt meant Meredith's goblet. His dad must have smashed it.

Then her mind put it *all* together. Mutt's eye. His sister. The ears on the stuffed dog. That domestic call, coming over her mother's radio and Mutt's dad, Mutt bragging about his service—

What else would Mutt do but this? She understood. And she didn't know what to say.

Bett thought again about how satisfying it must have been to break that glass over the transom, to smash that angel, and light the art aflame. Punching the river—she didn't say it out loud, but she should. She should tell Mutt she got it because it could have been her.

53

Autumn, Saturday, Early Morning

ALL OF THEM, SAVE MUTT, EXHAUSTED TO THEIR BACK teeth, climbed on Eddie's bus the next morning at six a.m.

Bett couldn't believe her mother was really making her go to this meet.

"I can't *hear!*"

"Oh, you're going," her mother said clearly. "I know you. Staying home in your room would be the treat. Not running that race. You don't need two ears to run. Besides, I have our friend Mutt's case to deal with later today, and I don't want you in my way."

She was brutal but right. Once again, she had Bett over a barrel two ways and Bett couldn't find a single argument, not even at all.

It was the weirdest bus ride Bett had ever taken, Mutt

missing and all of them potential criminals headed for lockup, or at least community service and ruined chances for college, and there was Eddie. "I heard about your antics and semantics last night," he said. "What's wrong with you yahoos? I told you we had a meet!"

"It was Mutt—" Dan started, but Eddie held up a quelling hand.

"Not until that kid gets his fair say," he said, and really, Bett was enough of her mother's daughter to agree.

"You all look scared shitless," Eddie said into the mirror as they drove away. "Don't be. This is our practice meet. Bett and Dan, you just keep your stride open and you'll be fine. Ranger, don't start out too quick or you'll get tired too soon."

The bus was silent.

"What are you all so quiet about?" cried Eddie.

"Don't worry. We have adrenaline," said Bett. "Believe me."

"Well, let's see it, then. Eat a PowerBar or something. I'm not bringing sacks of sand all the way over to compete in this meet."

"Who's this meet with anyway?" Dan asked.

Bett's eyes suddenly went wide. "Not Rayfen," she asked, suddenly feeling nauseated. How had she not considered the meet might be *there*? And what if her mother had told her father about it? Then her stupid father might stupid come—

"No," said Eddie, looking at her in the mirror. "Not them."

Thank God.

"It's Crow's Nest," Eddie continued, "because they're the ones who invited us, and that's where we're going. There might be one more school going as well. A triple meet. There was a question mark on the schedule."

Eddie drove like a mad thing over the roads made muddy and rutted from the rain.

"What the hell!" yelled Dan. "Baby on board, Eddie. BABY ON BOARD!"

"I'm not a baby!" yelled Ranger.

"I don't mean you!" Dan shouted back.

Anna snorted behind them. She wasn't supposed to run in this meet, obviously, because she had only had one practice, but they were going to sneak her in to get the right number of students from Salt River to count as a team. And Bett was on duty with Dan to wrangle Ranger. What with Mutt denying he had drawn them, Ranger's truthful, terrified little mouth couldn't be trusted not to start confessing all over the place and getting himself into trouble.

They rode along in silence, Bett worrying and worrying about how they were going to be punished for last night. Legally. Not just by having to do this meet. And when was her damn ear going to start working again?

Saturday, Meet Day

THEY FINALLY PULLED INTO THE CROW'S NEST SCHOOL parking lot. Bett gulped in a huge breath and let it out again.

"Don't be nervous," said Dan. Bett watched his lips carefully. "You're the best runner on this team."

Bett started.

"You are," he said. "You see anyone else getting chased with a bus?"

Bett smiled smally.

"Are your parents coming?" Dan asked her.

"You mean my mom? I doubt it. God, I hope not." That was all she needed, to have her mom shouting eighties cheers at her as she ran. But she figured her mother would be so busy getting ready to deal with Mutt that she wouldn't be able to come, anyway.

"Mine are," said Dan dismally.

"Just keep loose, Bett," said Eddie, talking at her in the mirror as he pulled the bus into its parking space. "This distance is nothing for you. You could do it in your sleep."

Bett nodded.

"All right, you twerps, we're here!" Eddie boomed, stopping the bus with a wake-up jar. "Stop the tiredfest and get focused on your running or I'm going to smack you all silly."

"You're not supposed to threaten us, Eddie," said Ranger wanly.

Bett needed her soda, needed the caffeine. She slipped it out of her backpack and took a sip, craning her neck to see out the window. Who was the other school?

And then she was choking. Coughing. Bett choked on the fizz, and the can flew out of her hand and soda was everywhere, can fallen on the floor, and Bett was out of her seat and pulling up the emergency handle on the back of the bus and out, flying down the road and running as fast as she could, running down this rutted awful road in front of the Crow's Nest school until she was far away, so far away that running was the only thing left.

Behind her the bus was still, growing smaller and smaller until Bett outran the sight of it over her shoulder and reared down a side road even bumpier and smaller than the one she left. Eff no Pluses. This running was no Plus. The other school was the Catholics, and guess who was getting off their bus.

Stephanie.

55

Saturday, Meet Day

THIS IS WHAT I GET FOR DOING A FIZZICLE FEET, BETT thought as she ran, with no need for Eddie to chase her with his bus. *This is what.*

A long, red, vintage Mustang pulled up beside her, a familiar face at the wheel—a guy with dark hair, so familiar but . . . grown, adult even.

Oh, my God, who is this?

It was Stephanie's brother, Bill. Of course it was.

"Bett!" Dan was calling her now from behind as he ran toward her. Eddie must have sent him, she thought. Dan? *Bill?*

"Bett!" Bill was rolling down his window and calling her from the side of the road.

Bett was trapped. There was nowhere to go. She stopped.

Bill leaned over and pushed the passenger door open. "Get in, Bett," he said. "I saw you jump off that bus. We got business."

Bett hesitated. Then she got in the car.

"Why are you even here?" Bett asked. Dan was still running down the road toward them. But Bill threw the car into gear, and as she and Bill passed Dan, Bett saw him peter to a stop and look back at the car.

Bill glanced at her. "I'm here to watch my sister," he said. "Why else? I don't have to be back at college until next week."

"Stephanie is doing cross-country? That's why she's here?"

Bill cocked his head. "All you need is two feet to run, Bett."

Two feet and one left eye.

Or two feet and one right ear.

But Bett didn't say anything aloud.

"Bill," Bett whispered, and Bill pulled over and parked the car.

"I know," he said, and pulled her into his arms.

Dan, jogging up to the car from behind, stopped, clearly having no idea what to do now.

"Excuse me," he said into the open window. "Bett, I don't know this guy."

"I don't anymore, either," said Bett, breaking into sobs. "I just cry on random people and get snot on them."

"To be fair, that happens when you laugh, too," said Bill, and Bett managed a chokey smile through her tears.

"Uh, Bett, um, we have a meet . . ." Dan obviously didn't know what to do with himself, and Bett didn't know what to do with him, either. Because Bill was right. She and he had business, and she had to take care of that. Most of what she had to take care of could happen after she ran this meet, after she was done and had run every word she had ever written on her soles and into her feet. But she and Bill had business now, and she had to take care of that first.

"Give me a minute? Five, tops?" Bett asked Dan. "Tell Eddie that my running out of the bus can count as my warm-up. I have to talk to Bill." She gestured back and forth between the two guys. "Bill, Dan, Dan, Bill." They chin-nodded at each other.

"Okay," said Dan. "But you'll miss walking the course. And don't miss your race. Eddie will go ballistic."

"I won't," promised Bett. But how could she run? She was suddenly just so damn tired.

But Bill was promising: "I'll get her there," and Bett knew he would.

As Dan jogged back to the school, Bill turned to Bett.

"First thing," he said, gazing levelly at her. "Why haven't you ever once come to see my sister? Not even once!"

Bett's body was on fire with remembrance.

"Bett—" Bill prompted her when she didn't respond.

"I couldn't. I can't."

"Why not?" Hard, firm.

"Because she was a perfect friend and a perfect human and I wrecked her. I wrecked her!" Bett burst out at last.

"No," said Bill. "Wrong. But put that to one side for a minute. Next: Why has she never gone to see you?"

Bett's head snapped up. "Why would she want to?" she asked, and here came those tears again. "It's my fault she lost her eye."

Bill stared at her. "Bett," he said, his voice cracking. "You *saved* her." His hands gripped the wheel so hard, Bett thought it might snap. "You broke her fall and rolled her away. She would have—Bett. You didn't . . . You saved her."

"NO!" cried Bett. She'd heard all this BS before. Her mother, Aunt Jeanette, the pastor. But she didn't, couldn't believe them. "I didn't! That explosion—it was all my fault! She hates me!"

"Are you kidding me?! *She* thinks *you* hate *her*."

"Why would I hate *her*?"

"Because our stupid mother fell for your stupid dad and wrecked your family."

"It's *my* stupid dad who fell for the Fl—your mom. And he wouldn't have if I hadn't blown up those gas pumps!"

"What?!" said Bill incredulously. "Hold on. Hold the hell on. There is too much here." He took one hand off the steering wheel and held up one finger. "First thing, who says it was you who blew up those pumps? One of the valves was so fragile it was about to blow at any second. That's what the insurance guy said."

"But *I'm* the one who made them do it," said Bett. "*I'm* the one who jumped on the hose."

"Trying to save my sister from her inept jump down our porch steps, I might add," said Bill. "Bett, anything could have made that gas pump burst."

"But *I* jumped on it. And it did burst."

"It did." Bill looked far away. Then his eyes were filling with tears, too. "We almost lost you both."

"I'm okay," said Bett. "Really. Who needs two ears?"

Bill smiled briefly, then got serious.

"Bett, you are not okay. You're not okay if the mere sight of my sister makes you run like hell down this road because you feel too guilty to—to . . ."

Be here.

Be.

But she wouldn't say that, although she knew it was true.

"If I hadn't encouraged Stephanie to do her Fizzicle Feet," Bett said carefully, "I wouldn't have jumped on that hose and there wouldn't have been an explosion and my dad wouldn't have shown up and fallen in love with your mom. He wouldn't have decided to leave me, I mean my mom, in, like, three days, the way he did. My dad would never have seen how gorgeous the Fl—your mom is."

"Oh, Bett," said Bill. "Come on. You're not that clueless,

are you? My mom. Your dad. They'd been having an affair for almost a year. Our parents blew up our families, not you."

What? What?!

But then, of course.

Of course.

The flowers. The phone call. The good-looking-dad comment from Stephanie, which must have been an echo of Mrs. Roan's own words. Bett's dad drawn to delicate and sweet, and surrounded at home by sturdy and competent.

Of course they had already been having an affair.

"Stephanie didn't get it either," Bill said. He shook his head. "She thought the same thing you thought. You two. So dense. You missed all the signs." He sighed and turned toward her again. "You understand now?"

Yes. But it didn't make a damn thing better.

56

Saturday, Just Before the Girls' Meet

As the only girls on the Salt River team, Bett and Anna had to share a locker room with the other visiting team.

Stephanie's team.

And there she was.

She had gone from pretty to gorgeous, her long dark hair shining in its ponytail, done up at the top with a clean blue ribbon like all the other girls on the Catholic team. She was still slight and tiny but more developed now, though not the way Bett was, which made sense, because Bett was pretty sure Stephanie didn't hide emergency Ho Hos in rock caves above the river.

Bett dug deep for the courage to speak.

"Stephanie," she said finally.

N. GRIFFIN

"Bett," said Stephanie.

They were silent. Bett wanted to look at Stephanie's false eye but couldn't.

"I hate your father," said Stephanie finally.

Bett's eyes went wide. That, she hadn't expected.

"I hate him, too," she said. "Also your mom. I hate her, as well."

"Oh, me too," Stephanie agreed. "I hate them both. Your father more, though."

"I get that," said Bett. "He's a twiddly little thing."

"He just doesn't ever shut up," said Stephanie. She was quiet. Then her whole body stiffened and she looked straight at Bett.

"I am so MAD AT YOU!" she cried.

Bett had been waiting for that. She forced herself to look into Stephanie's eyes. If Bett hadn't known one eye was pretend, she wouldn't have guessed it, but then Stephanie burst into tears and then Bett could tell, because although Stephanie had the same noisy weeping she'd had two years ago, tears came out of only one eye as she crarked like a crow.

"I'm sorry. I'm sorry!" Now tears were flowing down Bett's face, too, but from two eyes. Two.

"Why did you *never* come see me? I lost an *eye*, Bett! Why did you hate me for it? You never even called or texted or *anything*!"

"Hate you? Hate you for what? It was my fault!" Bett's

head was bent almost to her chest. "How could I face you when it was all my fault?"

Anna and the Catholics were gaping, yet trying not to gape. Then Anna nudged their captain and the girls moved away, letting Bett and Stephanie be alone.

"Your fault? What are you talking about?" shouted Stephanie.

"I stomped on that hose! *I* made the gas tank explode!"

"How stupid are you, Bett?" Stephanie cried. "That valve was ready to blow at any second—the insurance guy couldn't believe it hadn't already!"

"No!" cried Bett again. Stephanie was just echoing her brother and all the rest of them. "No!"

But this time was different.

"Yes." said Stephanie. "Yes."

Bett's left ear popped. She felt fluid trickle down her ear into her throat and the noise that came with it from the left was a surprise and too loud.

"I am so sorry, Stephanie." Bett's own voice boomed in her too-clear ear. "I am so sorry. I never hated you. Never."

"I hated you a little," Stephanie confessed, but before Bett could say anything, Stephanie added, "for abandoning me. With your father, of all people."

"I know. I know. I'm sorry. But I didn't hate you. I just didn't know what to do."

"I didn't, either. Maybe I should have called *you*."

"Why should you have when I avoided you this whole time?" Bett swept tears from her cheeks. "I'm so sorry, Stephanie! I'm so sorry!"

"So am I," Stephanie said. "You were my warrior Fizzicle Feet bestie, Bett."

"You were my beautiful-hearted best friend," Bett replied. "You're still beautiful."

"So are you."

"No, I'm fat."

"Not mutually exclusive, Bett."

"It is if you eat all the time until you're the size of a boulder."

"Who cares if you're fat? Who cares?" Stephanie cried.

The door to the locker room opened. It was the coach from the Crow's Nest team.

"Come on, girls," she said. "I don't know what drama you have going on in here, but you'll have to save it for later. The girls' race is starting."

"Wait—Bett—so—what are we?" asked Stephanie.

"I don't know," said Bett, wiping more wet from her face.

But she did know. One each of their selfish parents had made sisters of them.

And she tried not to cry again as they headed out for their race.

The gun went off, and off they went, Bett running like she hadn't run in years, her stride open and loose, no backpack to make it harder, but no choosing to stay still to take the Plus-feeling away, either. She owed it to Eddie to run. She'd been stupid, ignorant—thinking that war made all people crazy. She owed it to her team, who were in who-knew-what kind of trouble. She owed it to the fire of competition she couldn't hide in her heart. Did she owe it to Mutt? Oh, she didn't know. She couldn't think about that right now. She had to run.

The course was a double loop, just like the practice loop at home. There was a part that ran along a fence, and that's where all the spectators were. Bett saw Bill, then Dan and Ranger's mom and dad and, surprisingly, Paul there with his mother, and Eli, too. They must have come to show support for the Break-In Elite Force runners. And oh, no—Mom and Aunt Jeanette were there, too, after all, screaming, "GO, Bett! GO, Bett!" and Bett had to pretend she didn't see them as she pounded past.

The course wound through a narrow path in the woods, which was great, because it meant there was no way Eddie could chase Bett with the bus in here, even if he got mad at her. And he was mad. She passed him by the fence on the second loop and he screamed at her. "Get up GET UP *GET UP!*" and Bett moved faster until she thought she'd bust. She did it, though. Finished the second loop. Time 21:55. But she only came in second. One of the Crow's Nest girls was even faster.

But *No worries*, thought Bett. *I'll beat her next time.* She knew she could. And that she would.

* * *

Bett waited for Stephanie at the finish line. Stephanie came in second to last to Anna. Stephanie's time was 33:24. "I don't care," she said. "I just do it because I want to be more badass like you." And, just like in ninth grade, the two of them laughed until, again, they cried, now with Bett noisy as a crow and Stephanie's tears streaming out of her one real eye. And Bett didn't care if the laughing was ten thousand Pluses. She didn't care at all.

Once they got control of themselves, Stephanie said, "You know . . . your dad? He really wants to see you. Even if he is a twiddly jerk and won't shut up about self-reflection the whole time."

"I don't want to see him," Bett said quickly. "I'm not ready to forgive him."

"Oh, don't forgive him," said Stephanie. "Jesus, no. Just see him and let it suck."

Huh, thought Bett. *Huh.*

"Can I see you, though?" asked Stephanie. "Can I come *live* with you?"

Bett broke into laughter again. "You wouldn't believe where we're living now," she gasped. She laughed even harder, just as Bill walked up to them with his eyebrows raised.

"My mom built us a shack out of library books," Bett confessed, but before she could say more, the three of them were laughing and it was more pure Plus, blood coursing through Bett's veins and whispering to her:

Live.

HONK, HONK. That sound was familiar enough, anyway, although too loud in Bett's drained ear. The bus pulled up next to her. Eddie opened the doors. "Get the hell on my bus," he said. And Bett hugged Stephanie and Bill and got the hell on Eddie's bus.

An hour later everybody was gone except Eddie and Bett and the Eagles playing on the bus stereo.

"Eddie," said Bett. "Can we not have the Eagles the whole time now?"

"I don't know," said Eddie, eyes on the road. "You going to let me talk to you?"

Bett grew still. "Yes," she said finally. "I am."

57

Saturday, After the Meet

BUT HE DIDN'T START IN ABOUT HER WEIGHT.

"Two years ago. Driving up that hill." Eddie blew air sharply through his nose. "I was subbing your route that day. Christmas trees," he continued. "Cold. Kids were loud. Then your friend. That little girl. Jumping." Eddie shook his head.

So this was it.

Stop, Bett wanted to say. But she made herself listen, steeling herself for Eddie to tell her how he had seen Bett run toward Stephanie and land on the hose, bursting the tank. It was only what she deserved.

Eddie exhaled again.

"She hit that gas tank, Bett. The leaning one in the middle. Made it blow."

Bett was shocked into silence.

Then: "What? No. It was *me*. I ran over the gas hose. That's what made the pump explode."

Eddie shook his head. Blew air sharp again. "That's what I mean. Why I wanted to talk to you. I always knew you thought it was your fault." He paused. "I know you still think that. But it *wasn't* you. I've been wanting to tell you since August, when I saw your name on the sheet of kids for my bus. It wasn't you. Your friend fell against the tank, and that's when it exploded."

"No," said Bett.

"Yes," said Eddie.

"No," insisted Bett.

"You girls," said Eddie, voice cracking. "Flying. Falling."

Bett waited. Then Eddie pulled the bus to the side of the road because he had to see to drive, dammit, and could she quit distracting him.

Oh my God, Bett thought suddenly. *I was wrong, and this is the part where he kills me.*

"I just want to tell you one more thing," said Eddie.

"Okay," said Bett, and braced herself for the inevitable something about how she had changed and how running would slim her down and blah blah blah.

"I've wanted to say this since August, too," said Eddie. "I just want to tell you you'll always be safe on my bus."

Silence.

Bett broke it. "Except for when you stop short or kidnap us."

"Even then," said Eddie, and he turned and held out a hand to Bett. She took it and shook it awkwardly, and Eddie grasped her hand with both of his. "I never stopped thinking of you girls since that day. She okay?"

"Yes," said Bett, now crying. She had spent this whole day crying, and now here was more. "She is."

58

Saturday Evening

WHEN BETT FINALLY CAME IN, HER MOTHER AND Aunt Jeanette were already there. They'd left after Bett's race and not stayed for the boys' one. Dan and Ranger had done well, coming in sixth and tenth, respectively.

And now here were her mother and aunt, cooking soup like nothing was different.

"Is it true?" Bett demanded, still in her running gear. "Was Dad having an affair with the—with Stephanie's mom for a year before the gas explosion?"

Bett's mom stopped stirring. Bett knew she was shocked, not only at the question, but that Bett was asking it.

"Yes," her mother said finally. "It is true. How do you know?"

"Bill Roan. I saw Bill Roan at the meet and he told me." But even as she said it, Bett felt a dozen more puzzle pieces fall into place.

Mrs. Roan with not enough on.

Bett's dad bent over Stephanie.

He was bent over Stephanie after the explosion because he didn't know Bett was there. He had snuck out of the house to sleep with Stephanie's mother, so he was already there and he didn't know Bett was, too. That was why he had run to Stephanie and not her. That was why.

Oh my God, everything is different and nothing is different and everything in the world has exploded and I don't know how the pieces will come back together.

"You're welcome to call her the Floozy," said Bett's mom. "You know that language is permitted here in this home."

"No," said Bett. "It's not fair. If she's a floozy, then so is Dad. It takes two to tango."

Bett's mother stared at her. Then she snorted. "Believe what you will," she said. "Why do I make soup? I hate soup."

"So do I," said Bett.

Silence, except for the stirring pot.

"How did *you* know?" Bett asked finally.

"Took me a while," said her mother. "He kept going to the insurance office where she worked. I thought he was

straightening out something about our homeowners' policy, but no."

Bett shook her head.

"At least that's better than what *I* thought," said Aunt
Jeanette. "I swore he was taking out a policy on your
mother's life and was planning to do her in."

"That's ridiculous," said Bett, irritation at Aunt Jeanette
rising like a tide.

"It was," said Bett's mom. "But in a way it was true. His
leaving did do me in."

"Is that why you don't care if I don't see him? And why
he stopped coming to see me in the hospital?"

"He stopped coming because the twiddly little creep
chose that day to leave us, and he wanted to come to the
hospital to tell you, but I figured you had enough on your
plate."

"He did? He wanted to tell me in person?"

"Yeah," said her mother. "When you were deaf as a
post and *in the hospital.* And when I said he had to wait
until you were better, he told me I had to do it." She gave
the soup a ferocious stir so it sloshed over the sides of the
pot and hissed onto the burner of the stove. "The coward."

"MOM! You should have let him tell me!" said Bett.

Bett was suddenly furious with her mother. But she
hated her father more. Who left his family while his kid
was in the hospital? Would Bett ever stop hating him?

"I begged her, you know," Bett's mother said, not quite

looking at Bett. "I begged her not to take your father."

"I told you not to," said Aunt Jeanette.

"I had to," said Bett's mother.

There was a pause, and then she turned to face Bett. "But now," she said, "just so there are no more secrets: I'm dating your principal." And she moved away from the stove while Bett thought of the section of neck on Mr. McLean where he decided his beard ended and his chest hair could begin and felt physically ill at the thought that he would be spending time in the SIM card house and there would be no escape. What kind of day was this? Bett was suddenly too exhausted to even think about it.

"Ugh," she said to her mother, and went up the four stairs that led to her bed.

59

Saturday Night/Sunday Morning,
Wee Hours

DEEP NIGHT. BETT WAS AT THE TOP OF HER SLOPE AT the river's edge. There were no more cupcakes in her hidden cave.

Then she saw Hugh Munin, nightfishing at the bottom of the slope.

"I don't deserve . . . anything," said Bett, her own voice clear above the rushing of the river. What did Hugh Munin know? Why was she telling him this? Why did she want to so badly?

He heard her.

"You do," said Hugh. The light from the full moon spread out behind him on the water like a bulky coat, and even though it was time for them to roost, two grackles flew in and landed at Bett's feet, pecking the dirt in front of her.

60

The Following Friday

IT WAS NEARLY A WEEK LATER. THE SIX OF THEM—
Anna, Ranger, Dan, Hester, Paul, and Bett—involved in
the break-in were called into Mr. McLean's office, as well
as Mutt. Bett's mom was there, too, arms folded.

"We're letting the six of you who broke into the school
off with ten hours of community service each," Mr. McLean
said. "Mutt, you're facing more. Forty hours. Half of them
picking up trash on the sides of the streets. Half of them"—
he cleared his throat—"in the aftercare program in the elementary part of this building. And you'll be getting some
counseling, too."

Counseling, thought Bett. *Counseling.* Could she get
counseling, too? Should she? She imagined being in a quiet
room with Hugh Munin, inside, away from the river. His

kind eyes. *Counseling.* Maybe she should ask her mom.

"For the rest of you, I'm considering not entering this on your school records," he was continuing. "Though don't expect this kind of leniency for any new prank you brain trusts might think up. Or any other misbehaviors you might do the rest of the school year. One more thing happens, forget it."

"That statue," said Bett's mom, shaking her head.

Mutt lowered his head. "Do you think you can fix the statue?" he whispered to Anna, who was sitting in the seat beside him. "Like you did the other things? Please make something. Please."

Anna was silent. Then: "Yes," she said. "But not for you. But because I always, always will." And she folded her skinny arms across her chest and looked out the window as Mutt looked down at his hands beside her. "I'd make something out of those devil drawings, too, if someone would give them to me," Anna added, still looking out the window.

"That wasn't me, I swear!" cried Mutt.

Bett and Dan exchanged glances. Anna noticed and raised an eyebrow, as did Mr. McLean.

"Do I have official permission to do something to transform the statue?" Anna turned and asked him. "Please? And can I paint something over the graffiti stains in the entryway, too?"

"Yes," said Bett's mother, even as Mr. McLean was saying, "I'll give you a 'Maybe' about the graffiti. I don't know about the statue. We'd have to check with the town council. They're the ones who commissioned it."

"Oh, come on," said Bett's mother. "Let the kid fix the thing. It can't look worse than it does now."

Mutt lifted his head, and Bett understood something else. Because she'd been thinking about it, and it was starting to make sense. She got why Mutt had bashed the statue the same night the other kids were breaking in with the graffiti mural. It was the same reason he has done the other things so boldly during the day at school: Some part of him had wanted to be caught. As much as he said he'd done what he did because he wanted everyone to know he hated them, something in him craved help, too, for himself and his little sister.

Without thinking, Bett reached out and touched his arm. Why compassion for Eddie, who yelled and stopped the bus short, and not for Mutt? Why compassion for Mutt and not his father, who probably had some bad damn things happen to him, too? Why not compassion for all of them? How was she supposed to figure this out? Her head was spinning. What if the explosion *was* because Stephanie fell on the tank? Would Bett hate Stephanie for it? She wouldn't. She couldn't even imagine it, couldn't imagine ever even bringing up the possibility of blame. Not with Stephanie or with anyone.

"You kids better go," said Mr. McLean. "It's picture day and it's time for the juniors." He put his hand on Mutt's shoulder. "Dry your eyes and smile."

61

Not Long After on That Same Friday, In the Bathroom

CAREFULLY, BETT LINED EACH OF HER EYELIDS. SHE had already done her blush and lipstick, so all that was left to put on was eyeshadow and mascara.

"Can I borrow your eyeliner?" asked Paul.

"Sure," said Bett, and handed it over. Paul carefully dotted his nose and cheeks with fake freckles.

"I'm going for a country white boy look," he said to Bett, admiring himself from all sides. He was wearing overalls and a red tattersall shirt.

"I'm going for okay-looking," said Bett.

Paul slapped her hand, then held it. "Mission accomplished, lady. You look beautiful. But you always were."

62

Bus Ride Home, Friday Afternoon

MUTT'S EYES WERE DISTANT WHEN HE GOT ON THE BUS that afternoon. Bett sat down beside him.

"What the hell is up with him?" Eddie said out of the side of his mouth to Dan.

"You know what all's going on." Dan lowered his voice. "And what Mutt's dad is like."

Eddie shook his head, beating his steering wheel. "I'd like to punch that guy," he said.

So would I, thought Bett. *And I would like to punch me for not calling my mom about him that day in Fancy Jim's.*

The bus ride was silent, except for the Eagles.

Then, her mind made up, Bett turned to Mutt. "Listen," she said under the cover of the Eagles' "The Long Run." "I get it," she said.

"What does anybody get?" said Mutt. "People hurt people all the time and nobody understands. Might as well wreck everything before someone else does." He paused to wipe his nose on the back of his sleeve. "You don't get anything, Bett. Nobody does."

But Eddie had heard him. "Ha," he said. "You can't tell me I didn't go to war and see my buddies die, see buzzards circling over a dying girl's body, and I don't get it." His voice cracked, then steadied. "Made me mad as hell for years."

"You *don't* get it," said Mutt, his voice on the edge of breaking. "People just go on eating Ring Dings and holding fucking hands, running around a loop in a meet, and none of it makes any sense."

"Yeah," said Eddie. "That's what we do. But it matters. And a lot of us try to be good people, too. As best we can."

63

Saturday Night

Bett, Dan, Paul, Hester, and Anna were celebrating their community service punishment with a party, a party that was, given the hosts, full of Twinklers and Stays, gathering in laughing knots of themselves in Hugh Munin's field. It was like old Salt River times but better, somehow, Bett in her musty sweater, which she had decided this afternoon *was* cool and that she loved it. Stephanie was there, too ("Your makeup is amazing!" "I had this great teacher once."), as well as Ranger, shorter and younger than all the rest but ecstatic to be included. Both Dan and Bett had reinforced their threats to him about that stupid tufty-eared devil of whatever, and Ranger had looked sufficiently scared that they had trusted him to come along.

"This is a real partycakes!" he cried. "Are you guys going to drink stuff?"

"No," everybody chorused, and Paul and Eli put a cooler behind them.

Bett went over to Mutt, who stood on the periphery of the field. He was not exactly attending the party, but not exactly *not* attending it, either. Very few kids were forgiving of him. Most, like Dan, were still enraged.

"Are you scared?" she asked Mutt now. "About what might happen to you because of . . . ?"

"Yes," he said. "My parents . . . I need to get custody of Meredith when I turn eighteen," he said. "That's why I work so many jobs. I'm not letting her life be wrecked."

Wow. "I bet you could get help *now*," Bett said. "My mom says—"

"No," Mutt said vehemently. "'Help' is code for foster care, and no way. I'm not letting the police or the department of social services do that to us. My dad's a prick and my mother's useless, too, but I can take care of things for one more year, and then we'll be fine. I'll take classes at the community college after senior year while Meredith's at school during the day so I can be there for all the other stuff she needs when she comes home at five."

"Who'll take care of her until five?" Bett asked.

Mutt shrugged. "She goes to aftercare in the elementary wing most days, anyway." He smiled a little. Bett smiled back. Now she understood that part of Mutt's punishment.

"Forged my dad's signatures on the forms," Mutt added. "Nobody notices. I've had to do it for three years."

"Mutt," said Bett, "you are much less of a douche than I thought."

"No, I'm not," said Mutt. "I said homophobic, stupid shit, and I was an asshole to you on the first day of school, too. I'm sorry, Bett. I totally . . . respect what you can do."

"Thank you," said Bett.

"I'm going to head over to . . . the cooler. Can I bring you anything?"

"Nope," said Bett. "But thanks anyway." She watched him move through the group, some people ignoring him, some looking at him with pure disgust. Even most of his own minions were avoiding Mutt.

Bett shook her head. What was going to happen to him? To Meredith? Who could help them? Maybe her mother, who knew Mutt's situation. Maybe McLean. Bett shook her head hard. She'd have to think.

Someone had sparklers and was passing them from group to group, so the whole field twinkled like fireflies, like stars.

"What were you talking to Mutt about?" Dan asked Bett as they formed a tiny triangle with Stephanie in the midst of the party.

But Bett couldn't answer. And then there was Anna, buzzing up beside the three of them on her cricket-thin legs.

"Hey," she said to Stephanie. "I'm Anna."

"Hi," said Stephanie. "I'm Stephanie. This is Dan and Bett."

"I know them," said Anna. "We were recently arrested together."

Bett nearly spit-laughed. So did Stephanie.

"Bett is beyond the coolest, Anna," Stephanie said, and put her arm around Bett's waist. "Are you the Anna who made stuff out of the art that got messed up here?"

"I am," said Anna.

Stephanie's eyes went bright. "Whoa! Bett texted me a picture of the wings you made on the wall. They were gorgeous."

Anna grinned. "Thanks a lot. I just can't stand seeing destroyed stuff not made into something beautiful, you know?"

"Well, I make stuff as well," Stephanie told her. "Can I help with the statue? And maybe do something with the devil drawings, too?"

Oh, no. Bett hadn't had time to tell Stephanie the truth about those yet.

Anna looked at Bett and Dan. "What if Mutt *didn't* do those?" she mused. "He keeps saying he didn't."

"Of course he did," said Stephanie. "Fits the profile." And she slapped Bett's hand five for using cop language.

Bett felt a pang of guilt as she slapped Stephanie's hand, but then she thought of Ranger. *He's only twelve, for God's sake. And he thought he was helping. And Mutt's punishment—it wouldn't change even if Mr. McLean knew Mutt didn't do the drawings.*

"I'm not sure," said Anna, glancing at Bett and Dan again.

But Stephanie interrupted, "Your wings were so cool, Anna," she said. "What if—well, what about us making more and figuring out how to bronze them and getting them mounted on the statue?"

Anna's eyes went wide. "That's a fabulous idea. I bet the shop teacher would help us."

Dan was nodding enthusiastically. "I bet the whole shop class would. I could ask. We love that shit."

"And let's leave all the hatchet marks on the statue where they are," said Anna. "To represent the wounds the troops suffered. And what about vines growing out of one of the man's eyes? I'm addicted to these online videos that this girl in Rayfen does. She makes these insanely cool ones about these incredible Blythe dolls, and for one she made a flower and—"

Stephanie stopped dead. "Blythe dolls?" she said. "That's me! Those videos are me! I can't believe you watch them!"

"You are Rayfenetta? Oh my God! YOU ARE A GENIUS! Those dolls! They are the best!"

They *were* the best. Bett knew. Stephanie may have lost an eye, but Bett had certainly been keeping one on her through the Rayfenetta videos.

"Shut up!" cried Stephanie to Anna now.

"I will not shut up," said Anna.

"I'll make a doll just for you."

Bett blinked hard, embarrassed at the surge of jealousy she felt. Anna and Stephanie friends, too? But she tried to swallow it down and listened to the two of them talk, intense and focused with lots to say.

"Oh, I can't afford it," said Anna. "Don't call me a stalker, but I know how much your dolls go for on Etsy."

"Yeah, they're expensive. They'll put me through college," said Stephanie matter-of-factly. "But what if we just exchange work? Artist to artist?"

"Really?"

"Sure! What kind of doll do you want?"

"Can I have one you already made?" asked Anna. "The warrior with the woven metal breastplate?"

"No," Steph said unexpectedly. "Not that one. She's my Valkyrie . . . I am so sorry, but she's for Bett."

"A Valkyrie?" Bett said. The wisp of jealousy dissolved instantly. "For me?"

"Yup," said Stephanie. "Because you are my badass goddess sister."

Bett fought not to blush as her eyes welled. For a badass she sure had overwelling eyes. She and Stephanie slapped hands.

"Can I have the stone sprite with wings instead?" Anna asked.

"Sure. And I want something you make out of broken glass. I have a pile of it at home if you need it."

"Thank you," said Anna. "I feel like I'm in a dream. I'm collaborating with Rayfenetta."

Stephanie laughed. "I've never actually heard anyone say my handle out loud before."

Anna laughed back, and she and Stephanie continued to talk about their art and making things, hard and fast.

Ranger passed by, clearly not knowing what to do with himself. "Ranger"? Bett called to him. "Do you have a Sharpie?"

Ranger beamed. "I always do," he said, and handed it to her out of his hoodie pocket.

Bett tugged Dan down on the cold grass beside her and put one ankle on the opposite leg to write on the sole that Dan couldn't see.

COMPASSION, she wrote, and traced the letters until they felt permanent. And then over COMPASSION, she wrote PERMISSION. And beside the palimpsest of words she wrote TO SURVIVE.

Dan reached over and took the Sharpie from Bett. And, hoisting his own foot over his knee, he wrote four letters on his sneaker sole.

Bett swallowed. She was not going to presume.

Dan sighed. "Don't make me say 'I like you, Bett.' It'll make me feel like I'm Ranger's age."

Bett was surprised into silence. Dan's face fell.

"I mean, I know you probably like that Bill guy," he said hastily. "I remember you wrote his name on your sneaker when we were younger."

"You noticed that?" said Bett, now doubly surprised.

"You used to stick your feet up on my desk all the time when we did that Social Studies project in ninth grade," said Dan. "I saw a lot of shit you wrote on those sneakers."

Then Bett raised the other foot, the one that Dan could see, and wrote three letters on that one.

"Ranger," Dan called out, "why don't you go get one of those sparklers?"

"Okaycakes," said Ranger, and fairly ran to the girl distributing the sparklers. He took one and dashed as far away from Dan and Bett as he could.

NOW

BETT BROUGHT STEPHANIE AND THE OTHERS OVER TO the basement hole where they had planned the Art Attack and where Eddie had thrown Mutt's phone, and they all crawled down inside to look around. But now Bett was pulling Stephanie back out of the hole, hand over wrist and up over the lip. The others followed and then all seven of them beat it up the rest of the dirt slope and ran—streaked it across I Know a Guy Field like coyotes were chasing them, and Bett loved it, the words on her soles pounding into every beat of her heart, overlapping the beats just as they overlapped on her feet. The seven kids flew across the street and paused at the top of the slope to the river. Of course Hugh Munin was down there in his waders, night-fishing. But clumps of kids were dotting the shore here and there, too, and now the seven of them were up here, Bett leading them, and she was ready, ready to jump high off the slope so it felt like flying to burst and land amidst the kids down there making cairns and doing who knew what else, but it didn't matter because Bett was there, ready to take Dan's hand and fly down the slope to the rushing water below and let things happen next.

"... Woden took nine twigs of glory, and then struck the adder so it flew into nine. There archived apple and poison that it would never re-enter the house."

—adapted from Bill Griffith's translation of *The Nine Herbs Charm*

Acknowledgments

There are always so many people to cherish and thank in the making of a book. Here is who I cherish and thank for this one: Caitlyn, Linda, Ariel, Kristin, Tobin, Adrienne, Ann, Jen, Kelley, Allen, Jane, Darsa, Miriam, Hannah, Susan, Lana, MaryAnn, Bridie, Tate, Coco, Elana, Samantha, Carol P., and Leah W.

Skint's in the Pit because of Dinah. So she figures she better get cracking and affect his speedy release. Dinah would go to the **ends of the earth and back** if it would help Skint.

But is it possible to try too hard to save your best friend?

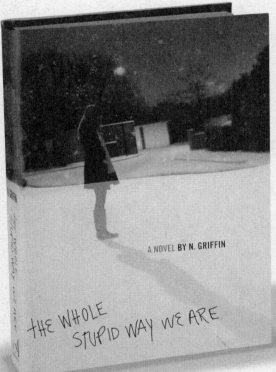

A NOVEL **BY N. GRIFFIN**

THE WHOLE STUPID WAY WE ARE

"So furious, so heartbreaking. . . . A thing of beauty, that's what this is."
—Kathi Appelt, author of
The Underneath, a Newbery Honor book

Learning not to drown.

A novel by Anna Shinoda.

The prodigal son is about to stretch Clare's family to its breaking point.

A gripping debut novel that cuts right to the bone and brings to life the skeletons that lurk in the closet.